Sherlock Holmes and the Secret of the Three Monks

By Johanna M. Rieke

First English edition published in 2021
© Copyright 2021 Johanna M. Rieke
First published as 'Das Geheimnis der Drei Mönche' in 2014 in Frankfurt, Germany, by Public Media-Verlag

The right of Johanna M. Rieke to be identified as the author of this work has been asserted by her in accordance with the Copyright, Designs and Patents Act 1998.

All rights reserved. No reproduction, copy or transmission of this publication may be made without express prior written permission. No paragraph of this publication may be reproduced, copied or transmitted except with express prior written permission or in accordance with the provisions of the Copyright Act 1956 (as amended). Any person who commits any unauthorised act in relation to this publication may be liable to criminal prosecution and civil claims for damage.

Although every effort has been made to ensure the accuracy of the information contained in this book, as of the date of publication, nothing herein should be construed as giving advice. The opinions expressed herein are those of the author and not of MX Publishing.

Paperback ISBN 978-1-78705-693-0
ePub ISBN 978-1-78705-694-7
PDF ISBN 978-1-78705-695-4

MX Publishing, 335 Princess Park Manor, Royal Drive, London, N11 3GX
www.mxpublishing.com

Cover design by Brian Belanger
Translation by Bryan Stone

For Bryan, my dear husband,

who is the great love of my life

After the Thames Murders

For the criminologist, the year 1890 had up to April shown no particularly unusual features of interest. At that point, however, London, as you, dear reader, may recall, was shaken by a series of murders. There seemed to be no common features, apart from the fact that the victims were killed in an extraordinarily bestial manner, and that the murders were all committed in a district on the south bank of the Thames, opposite the Isle of Dogs. This led to the press and public giving them the name of "The Thames Murders," and so they are now known. I had come to concern myself with this affair only in June, as my newly started practice in Kensington demanded my full attention. Moreover, since I was now married, the little free time I could enjoy was spent with my dear wife, Mary. I saw therefore little of my friend Sherlock Holmes, but as summer came on, and the practice was less busy, I offered to help Holmes in his enquiries into the background of the Thames murders. At the risk of our lives we identified the murderer, and so ended his evil career, and were able to frustrate a plot which, had it succeeded, would have cost many innocent lives. I may here say no more, for the involvement of our present government in the matter obliges me to maintain silence in respect to the details. I can only say that it was, for me, by far the most dramatic experience that I had ever shared with Holmes. Knowing, dear reader, what dangers we had in earlier cases sometimes had to face, it will not come as a surprise, that we both paid a price for our final success. Both Holmes and I were wounded, in a final confrontation with our opponent, and had to spend some time in hospital, before Holmes went back to 221B Baker Street to recuperate in the care of the landlady and housekeeper, Mrs. Hudson, while I went with my Mary to convalesce in the Sussex countryside.

Mrs. Forrester, of London, by whom Mary had been employed as a companion up to our marriage, invited us to her country home by Robertsbridge, in East Sussex. This generous gesture may be more readily understood, when I explain the relationship of these two ladies. As Mary, after the unexplained disappearance of her father, Colonel Morstan, became an orphan, left to her own resources, she entered the service of Mrs. Forrester. Mary had thereby not only the opportunity to earn her own living, but she also found in Mrs.

Forrester a loyal, almost motherly, friend, who became devoted to her. This benevolent concern for her well-being did not end with our marriage, although their contacts now were necessarily restricted to correspondence. Mrs. Forrester had however several times invited Mary to spend some days with her in Sussex, and so it came about, as she learned of my wounds, that she readily extended the invitation to both of us, to stay with her during my convalescence. Mary gladly accepted this invitation, and so we found ourselves, on June 19th, leaving London by train for Robertsbridge, a village some 10 miles north of Hastings. On arrival at the station in Robertsbridge, we found the pony and trap awaiting us, for the remaining three miles to Mrs. Forrester's country house. She came out to greet us, and had soon led us to our room, where we unpacked our luggage. There followed most agreeable and relaxed days, during which I felt my strength returning. I was soon ready to face the future without anxiety, and to devote myself again to my patients and to my wife.

It was however not long before I noticed how often I thought of Holmes, and wondered how he was faring. Inevitably I became more concerned as time went by, not however because of his injury, for I could trust his robust constitution and his strong will to take care of that. My concern was much more, what he was now doing, especially since I hoped, if he had a new case to solve, that he would properly take care of himself. But much more disturbing was the thought that he might have no new case to occupy him, as I knew all too well, from the time I shared with him in Baker Street, the phases through which he might be passing. At first he would be like a restless, caged animal, pacing back and forth. There then followed outbreaks of irrational anger, which were mostly directed at his housekeeper, poor Mrs. Hudson. Finally he would then draw in on himself, give no more regard to person, appearance or sleep, and play discordantly on the violin for hours on end. In the worst case there was another phase which might then follow, when he would look for his needle and cocaine, make up a seven-per-cent solution, and inject it to try to animate his wits. This thought tormented me. I had on several occasions, as his friend and doctor, made clear to him my strongest objections; but it seemed to have made no impression. I failed miserably in my attempts to convince him that the stimulation, which he found in the drug, came at a fearful cost in his body and spirit. For him, the cocaine injection was the substitute for the stimulation he otherwise found in meeting the challenge of a difficult problem which required his full concentration.

I was so concerned that I decided to write to Holmes and to describe to him some of the features of our stay in Robertsbridge. That was of course not something which he would find particularly interesting, but it might at least occupy his mind and distract him from his extreme solution.

My first letter to Holmes

Robertsbridge, 29 June, 1890

My dear Holmes,

Ten days have already passed, since you left me with Mary at London Bridge station, as we took the train which would take us to Robertsbridge. After a good journey we were made welcome most hospitably, at Mrs. Forrester's house, which lies north of Robertsbridge and stands alone in the country. Her land is bordered on the east side by a stream, and on the south side by a track which leads into the old London road, leading first to the small village of Etchingham, northwest from us. There are here no immediate neighbours, but Mrs. Forrester maintains friendly relations with a family living two miles south of Robertsbridge, that of Richard Welling, a business person who has a factory manufacturing various kinds of printing ink near Hastings. Alongside his property there is, on the east side of the road to Battle and Hastings, a narrow road which leads to the Old Abbey, a former monastery. If this name seems curious, it is in

Robertsbridge necessary, for there were here two abbeys, of which however the old one is completely ruined and in a parlous state.

As you see, I have already acquired a certain knowledge about this district. I might almost say that I was obliged to learn, but you might form your own opinion about this. I came by my knowledge shortly after our arrival here, when the local vicar, Reverend Samuel Crane, paid a visit to Mrs. Forrester. He had heard that a London doctor, with his wife, was visiting, and could not resist the opportunity to have what he called a "cultivated conversation," which he seemed to miss in his daily affairs. When he heard my name, however, he could not hold back his admiration. You, Holmes, were praised for your tireless battle for good, and I was praised for my exciting accounts in the "Strand" magazine. Be assured, my dear friend, that in Reverend Crane you have an enthusiastic admirer of your deductive skills, and it has become clear that he is therein not alone. I will enlarge on this later. It suffices to say that I was taken by his sympathy, and, at his insistence, told him something of our lesser adventures. There came, inevitably, the moment where he felt obliged to share with me some of his extensive knowledge of Robertsbridge. So it was that he embarked upon a lengthy, and exhausting, account about the village and its abbeys. While he was talking, apparently without stopping to draw breath, it occurred to me that I might have been spared this history lesson, had I not allowed the good vicar to address me as the friend and companion of that man whom he so much admired. It is therefore perhaps my duty to pass on to you at least an outline of the information he wanted to share with us.

The first abbey, the one that is here known as the 'Old,' was endowed in 1176 by Richard, he who would in 1178 become King Richard I of England. It was a subsidiary monastery of Boxley Abbey, a Cistercian abbey, of which the first Abbot was Robert de St. Martin. He gave his name to the first bridge over the river Rother. In 1197 the Abbots of Robertsbridge and Boxley went to search for England's lost King John, whom they in fact found, in Bavaria, the southern part of Germany. During their long absence it became clear that the Abbey had been built in an unsuitable location, and was constantly under threat of flooding. In 1250, therefore, the Abbey was abandoned. A new abbey, nearer to Salehurst but still known as Robertsbridge, was built. This became clearly a greatly respected house, for both King Henry III and King Edward II visited it. By the end of the 14th Century, however, it was declining, and at the time of the Dissolution in 1538, there were only twelve monks in residence. The land was later sold off to Sir Philip Sidney, who used it for secular purposes and even installed a blacksmith's workshop, a smithy. With the end of his family line, however, it was also left to become a ruin.

At this point our conversation was interrupted by the appearance of Mrs. Forrester and Mary, who brought in tea and biscuits, so that the vicar chose to break off his account in order to concentrate with obvious enjoyment on this refreshment. After tea, he was anxious to take his leave, as soon as politely possible, because, as he said, he still had to prepare his sermons for the next Sunday's worship.

After this rather exhausting visit, I was pleased that the next few days were quieter. I found a need to sleep deeply during the day, and was pleased to use the couch which was placed in the garden for me. At intervals I went for a walk with

Mary, though we scarcely needed to leave the grounds, as my weakness showed itself with every physical effort. Nevertheless, I felt the benefit of the quiet and rest, as my strength came back, and I could walk further. I have also been fishing, though with modest success. Yesterday evening Mr. and Mrs. Welling came to visit. I was greatly impressed by their friendly and helpful manner, and by the respect and affection they displayed for one another.

After dinner the ladies withdrew and I sat with Mr. Welling in the study of the late Mr. Forrester, to enjoy a pipe and a whisky with him. It was not long before we began an animated discussion about various criminal cases. Mr. Welling is, like the vicar, an enthusiastic admirer of your deductive capacities, and it would surely be his fond wish to meet you personally. This was obvious from the warmth and engagement with which he spoke, and I therefore allowed myself to suggest that, when he is in London, he should take the opportunity to call at 221B Baker Street. I hope this is not unwelcome to you. He also laid great value on my literary description of some of our cases. As I feared that this might become an unending eulogy, I succeeded in diverting our conversation to him and his affairs. He has, as I noted above, a factory, making printing ink. Hastings is not itself a port, but Mr. Welling does export some of his specialised products to the Continental mainland. It seems that this is not easy, as transport costs, import duties and occasional damage to his barrels are all to be overcome; but the quality is itself convincing, and allows him some time to resist the efforts of his foreign competitors. He was, as I understood, very relieved when, two years ago, Her Majesty's Stationery Office and the Royal Mint became his clients. He laughed to tell me that not only our adventures in the "Strand Magazine," but also many share certificates, official documents and even our five-pound-notes are printed with his ink.

As we then returned to join the ladies, we found them also engaged in conversation. Mrs. Welling had, as Mary told me late at bedtime, spoken most affectionately of their son, Robert. This boy is ten years old, and had until recently lived at home. The parents felt, however, that this was not now the best for him. He had in Robertsbridge no friends or companions, apart from his dog, Chelsea, a devoted Sussex Spaniel. With only adults for company, he was almost always alone. His parents felt that his healthy development needed more, and so they had placed him, also after some hesitation, in a small boarding school near Tonbridge. This school was well spoken of, and made a good impression, and Tonbridge is only twenty miles from Robertsbridge, with a direct rail line.

Mrs. Welling did not conceal that this had caused her considerable pain, as she took leave of her son. She had seen that it was no less painful for Mr. Welling, but they would soon be able to welcome Robert at home. The school holidays began in July, but the Headmaster had suggested that Robert should come home a few days earlier, after suffering from a mild influenza, harmless but needing care. He thought it might be better to send Robert home. It was arranged that they would surprise Robert and together fetch him with the carriage on July 2nd.

Mary and I had the feeling that Robert Welling, as far as he took after his parents, was surely a most likeable child. Well, next week we shall see for ourselves.

You will see, therefore, my dear friend, that I am making the most of my time in this idyllic and quite sleepy rural district. I hope you have also now made a good recovery, and are now finding new challenges to occupy you.

Until we again meet, and with all good wishes, from your old friend

John Watson.

P.S.: *Mary wishes me to send her kind greeting to you, and this I gladly do.*

My second letter to Holmes

Robertsbridge, 3 July. 1890

My dear Holmes,

It will surely surprise you to receive so soon a further letter from me. In the meantime, however, events have taken a most puzzling and very troubling turn, and I have been obliged to think again of my picture of Robertsbridge and of its people. Calm and tranquillity have been replaced by threats and fear. It may be that all can be explained, and that I am unnecessarily and unduly concerned. Perhaps you, my friend, may see an explanation, so that I allow myself, in this hope, to give you a chronological account of these events.

Mrs. Forrester had told me that in the parish church there is exhibited a unique and historic music manuscript of the 14th century. I therefore determined to visit the church this morning, to see this exhibit. I met again the vicar, who was only too pleased to accompany me and to show it personally to me. Reverend Samuel Crane is the vicar of Salehurst, to which parish Robertsbridge belongs, and was clearly well-versed in the culture and history of Robertsbridge, for he again delivered a detailed account of the document and its significance. It is considered to be a musical manuscript of about 1360. It is indeed unique and is believed to be the earliest manuscript written to display music for a keyboard instrument. In the music world it is known as the Robertsbridge Codex.

The vicar might have continued, but then at twelve his attention turned to his lunch, which was waiting at home. He did invite me to join him, but my need for his garrulous hospitality was already satisfied, and I needed no more. I therefore declined politely, pleading an appointment with the Wellings. Should you be interested in the Robertsbridge Codex, I have learned that it is not necessary to come here; the vicar told me that the exhibit in his church is a copy, and that the original is in the British Museum in London. Knowing that, I might have spared myself a visit to the church and my meeting with the vicar.

I walked a little later along High Street, where the village houses are mostly of the 14th century. Not only the architecture betrays this, but much of the material is also of the period, and was recovered by the villagers of that time as the first abbey was abandoned. This was so well done that everywhere stones and arches can be found, silent witnesses of that far-off earnest but sometimes disreputable time. Walking southwards I came to the Wellings' house, and, as I was uncomfortable about my mild dishonesty with the vicar, I resolved to call in, although unannounced, and thus have an opportunity to ask Mrs. Welling about her son.

She received me in the drawing room, where I at once felt, despite the warmth of the summer's day, that there was a bitter chill in the room, which left me inexplicably shivering. The windows were all shuttered, so that no sunshine could enter. But this was not the only reason why I felt so uncomfortable in this room. Mrs. Welling, whom I had only recently seen as most good-humoured, was now very withdrawn and quiet, indeed, almost hostile. Her greeting was courteous, but her friendliness seemed contrived. As I then asked how her son had enjoyed his time in boarding school, I saw how her body stiffened, and her eyes seemed to fill with tears. Her right hand, clenched to a fist, went to her mouth, and she bit into her finger. The pain seemed to bring her back to my presence, for she suddenly looked at me like a hunted animal, stood up sharply, and with a muttered "Excuse me," fled from the room. I had risen, and now stood alone in the drawing-room. Propriety forbade me to follow a lady, but I was deeply concerned by this behaviour.

Before I could make any decision, however, there entered one of the house staff, who informed me that the lady of the house felt unwell, and that my visit should be postponed until later. I was correctly but firmly shown to the door. There, however, I almost collided with Mr. Welling, entering the house. He also greeted me correctly, but with reserve. He asked me my business there, and I very properly described my wish to ask after their son. His reaction was, if not as dramatic as that of his wife, at once obvious, and I saw him become pale. As I described how his wife's indisposition had troubled me, I saw his eyes narrow, and the pupils searched for a safe hold. Then he clenched his fists, until the knuckles were starkly white. Red patches flamed in his cheeks, and I half feared an outbreak of angry rage. Then, suddenly, he relaxed, and with an effort tried to tell me that Robert had in some way caused trouble at school, and that he was therefore no longer to be allowed to come home early. I would, of course, understand that they were, as parents, not pleased, and his wife had taken it badly as she thought so highly of Robert. This explanation was plausible, and it caused me naturally some grief to know that I had unwittingly caused such pain. I apologised, and left the house with the usual courtesies.

As I left, I could not but reflect, how different was the impression these nervous and highly distressed persons had made on me, and what might have happened, that the friendly and cheerful couple which I had only four days early come to know, might be so completely disturbed. Had Robert's shortcomings really provoked such a change, and if so, what might he have done? The shock I had experienced troubled me, and I needed a moment's rest. I walked back to the High Street to where a narrow street branched off to the east, and crossed an old bridge over a deep stream. On the other side the path led to the ruined remains of the Abbey. It seemed good and inviting to walk up to the ruins, but as I crossed the bridge I heard a thin wailing sound. Following the sound, I found an older lady, dressed in black, under the bridge. I looked more closely, and saw her fall on her knee and drop a small wreath of flowers into the fast-flowing water. Then she began to sing a nursery song, her body rocking gently to the melody.

I had at first thought that she needed help, but it seemed rather, that she was following a ritual. Feeling myself an intruder, I did not wish to disturb her, and made to draw back. She had seen me, however, and spoke to me, but in such a confused manner, that I could not follow or summarise her meaning. I try therefore to record here the expressions she used.

"God bless you, stranger, who are you, what are you doing here?"

"My name is Watson. My wife and I are visiting Mrs. Forrester for a few days. I thought that on this fine day I would visit the ruins. And whom have I the pleasure to meet, Madam?" While I spoke to her, her stare was fixed on the

water in the river. She was perhaps between forty and fifty years of age, but her emaciated and bent body, and her white hair, made it very difficult to be sure. She ignored my question and suddenly spoke again.

"I've brought some flowers for my little Georgie, but I don't know if he really wants flowers, where he is in Heaven, surely the flowers there are much more beautiful than here, don't you think so, sir?"

This confused speech and her wide eyes betrayed to me that she was either drugged with opiate, or that she was seriously mentally disturbed. I tried to find an answer which might fit her condition. "In any case, I am sure that your Georgie is pleased to have your flowers."

"Yes, sir, I think so, he was always such a dear child, and he still is. Just a short time ago he rescued me, as the devil came after me with a carriage."

This woman awoke my sympathy, and I tried to carry the conversation further, however curious it might turn out to be.

She had surely often seen people turn away to leave her in distress; some were surely even afraid of her. So I asked her further: "How did your Georgie rescue you?"

"It was the night before last, I was here to sing my Georgie to sleep, you see, sir, he was always afraid of the dark.... And as I was singing, I heard the clatter of hooves, just above me, like the riders of the Apocalypse, coming to destroy this sinful place. But then I heard the clatter of the carriage, and I knew that the devil himself was after me, He catches poor souls, you know, and loads them into his carriage, and when it is full, they go off to hell."

Although it was clear to me that this outburst from the poor woman betrayed a severely disturbed fantasy, I asked again, "And you think the devil was after you?"

"Indeed he was, sir, I heard the wild beat of the devil's hooves on the old boards when the carriage stopped just over me. Then there was a fearful scream, a terrified shout for help. I thought my Georgie was calling me from the water to save him, but then I knew, he was calling his angels from heaven to

save me. I fell on my knees and gave up prayer after prayer. I felt weak, and then everything around me went black, and I must have lost my senses. I woke up lying on the bank here, cold but unharmed."

"And the devil and his carriage? What was become of them?" I asked.

"They were naturally gone, but then, sir, we know that even the devil cannot prevail against the might of the angels and the prayer of a devout soul." During all this she had become more animated and became increasingly fanatical, and these were symptoms which, as I well knew, belonged to such an affliction. I felt I had to do something for her, and suggested: "I am going back to the village. Would you like to accompany me?"

"No, thank you, sir, I must stay a while with my Georgie." With these words she was already swaying her body and started singing her nursery song. She was again in the ritual in which I had first found her. I knew from

experience that there was no way of again taking up the contact, and so I turned back, rather chastened.

A short walk brought me to the most prominent, and obviously historic, public house in the village, the Seven Stars Inn, and I determined to step inside to accord myself a quiet whisky. I knew it was needed, and the landlord, one Peter Hunt, had obviously seen so too, for he said so without hesitation. However, I also learned a few points I considered worthwhile, so I will try to bring them for you here. I emptied my glass as Mr. Hunt observed, "Forgive me, sir, but I felt you needed that. You looked very shaken as you came in. Another? It's not so good, standing on one leg!"

"Oh, no, thank you," I answered, "but a glass of beer would be good. And draw one for yourself."

"Thank you, sir, one recognises the gentleman from the big city! You must be the visitor at Mrs. Forrester's."

"I am indeed."

"I thought so as you came in. Here we all know one another. And a stranger who is generous, that must be the visitor from London!" He felt he must explain. *"Sir, you must forgive us, here in the country. When one of us hears something new, then soon we all know. As soon as the vicar knew that you are the friend of the famous detective, Sherlock Holmes, the word went round very quickly."*

"I quite understand. But excuse me, Mr. Hunt..."

"Peter, sir. That is what we all say, here."

"Peter, then, as you are surely well-informed, you must know a woman around 45, with white hair, whom I saw under the bridge leading to the abbey."

"Yes, that is Esther Brown. She is the wife of George Brown, the grocer, who keeps the general store."

"She talked about Georgie. Do you know who that could be?"

"Naturally, that was her son, little George, who was drowned there under the bridge, why, it must be fifteen years ago. He was only nine when he died, He was always playing by the ruins and under the bridge, although he shouldn't have done. One day there came a sudden rush of water, and he lost his footing and fell. It was a dreadful blow to Esther and George."

"I can well imagine".

"And Esther has always reproached herself, and you know, sir, one should not talk badly of the people, but she was always after the money. She worked in the shop to avoid having to engage another helper, and she was determined to have enough money to pay for Georgie to have a good education and a good future. Since she was then rarely at home, Georgie was left to himself. On his death, she took all the responsibility on herself, and we feared she might even drown herself. But she read a lot in the Bible, and seemed to have taken hold again. But she is often, well, rather unusual."

He was interrupted by two other customers, and I had a moment to reflect. The chattering of the poor woman had now at least a certain meaning, and my sympathy was awakened. There was also, however, that sense of helplessness which comes with realising, as a doctor, that little can be done for such a case. Peter returned, and continued his remarks, saying that old George could have sent her into an institution but he refused. He said that he had sworn to look after her, in good and ill, and that he would do. Then he kept her at home, but she would always slip out to go to where her Georgie died. "Yes, sir, it is indeed tragic, but.... Will you have another glass?"

I was not ready to walk back, and let him fill the glasses again. I was thinking of my time as a young medical student, with an obligation to work for three months in a mental institution. The conditions there were for me quite inhuman, and some of the treatments which were tried, on helpless and confused patients, seemed quite barbaric. Although it was a short stay, I could not comply with these practices, and made such a protest that it might have cost me my qualification. By good fortune I won the support of my mentor, Dr. Bell, in

Edinburgh, who supported me energetically. But Peter came back again.

"And something else, sir, have you seen the three monks?" I looked at him with surprise. "Obviously you haven't, but now that it's just past full moon, last Sunday, they always appear on the little hill by the road to the Abbey ruin."

"You said, three monks?" I said sceptically.

"Yes, sir, naturally not three ordinary monks, but the ghosts of the last three monks at the Abbey. The story is that they were attacked by a band of trouble-makers, and were so ill-treated and beaten, that they died." The landlord had become unusually serious, and spoke with an earnest expression which gave his words their fullest effect. I had to suppress any tendency to smile or even laugh. I tried to give the impression, so as not to be scornful, that I really wished to know more, so asked if he had seen them himself. "Oh, yes, sir! They are three monks in white habits, who walk over the hill, and swing the torches in their hands."

"I see, and when do these monks appear?"

"Only at night, and especially just at the full moon, and sometimes in the nights after the full moon, but never when the new moon is in the ascendancy. Then it's over, for another month"

"And how long can you see them?"

"That, sir, can be very different. It can be short, but I've heard that it can be two hours. No-one really likes to say, because they are said to be cursed, No one wants to stay near, because awful things can happen. There was old Thomas Kyle, a while back, a respectable man, strong as an ox, had a barn over there behind the hill. He ignored the warnings of others, said he didn't believe all that, and went off to repair the barn roof. And what do you think happened? A thunderstorm came up suddenly, and he was struck by lightning, dead on the spot."

I needed to say nothing, because he went on to tell me of other misfortunes which were attributed to the monks' appearances. But all at once he broke off and smiled. "But even a curse can have its good side, even for me! When the people here are frightened, they hold together and look for company, and then they come in here. If they don't go out, but come into the inn, then I can see the monks as a blessing." With that, he laughed, and we clinked our glasses once more, before I left to walk back to Mrs. Forrester's house.

She and Mary were waiting for me, as I had been out a long time. And now, as I have written this account at length over the events of the last few days, I ask myself if it is right to burden you with them. Perhaps I have attached too much importance to things of no account. That can easily happen when one has too much free time. I sincerely wish that you were here to share with me, and to quiet my disturbed mind, which is all too ready to suspect the worst!

Tomorrow, Mary and I plan to accompany Mrs. Forrester, taking the train for a two-day visit to Hastings, This diversion may help to settle my uneasy mind.

In the meantime, as always, your friend, *John Watson*

The Gypsy

The outing to Hastings did indeed help to calm my anxiety. Mrs Forrester spent much of the daytime with her friends there, leaving Mary and me to make long walks on the almost three-mile-long beach. As, on one of our walks, the tide came up, it left only a narrow strip of sand above the waterline, and we wondered how the many fishermen here could dry their nets.

As if in answer, as we walked along the many wooden huts along the beach, the high doors of one of them opened, and we saw how the nets were hung up inside. We even learned that the cabins were known as net-shops, and that they are a well-known feature. We also walked along the pier, and enjoyed the air and the sunshine. Although full of activity, with fishermen and dealers, there was an air of calm and quiet.

On the first evening, we played bridge with Mrs. Forrester's friends, but on the second evening there was a public lecture, on the Fauna and Flora of Australia. This was the idea of Mrs. Forrester, who had a great interest in that far-away continent, of which so little is known. The late Mr. Forrester had spent some early years in Australia, and had always spoken so positively of it that she still felt much sympathy. The opportunity to learn more was too good to miss. I was at first unsure whether it was an appropriate venue for ladies, but I had to admit that the presentation was both successful and interesting. We were not only shown examples of dried plants and stuffed animals, but enjoyed a lively visual presentation of this strange continent, by magic lantern, with pictures so lifelike, both of animals and of native persons, that one felt near enough to reach out.

As we returned to Robertsbridge by local train, on Sunday, 6 July, the concerns which had preoccupied me in the previous days were gone. The train stopped first at Battle, the small town which marks the site of the famous Battle of Hastings, in 1066, when the Normans invaded England. Arriving at Robertsbridge, we found we were the only passengers to alight. As it had just begun to rain, we were in haste to take our place in the waiting carriage. However, I could not but notice a disreputable figure, by appearances a Gypsy, lounging around the station house. He had a battered hat, of which the brim was broken through, and as a hatband this garment had around it a knotted cord. Although I could not see clearly, there seemed to be feathers, chicken bones, crows' feet and a hare's foot on the cord. Long, greasy and knotted hair hung down, and his deeply brown, swarthy face sported a long, flowing but unkempt black beard, and bushy eyebrows, with treacherous shifty eyes. Around his neck was a once yellow cloth, with black spots. The red shirt and the trousers, as far as one could see, were full of torn patches, and his sleeves were turned back so that we saw his filthy arms. Around his wrists were leather thongs, and he had a brown jacket of some kind of animal skin. The last details I noticed of this most unappetising person, were his high boots, the leather cracked and torn, and where, through the lace holes, a length of dirty string was threaded.

I felt that he had, without approaching, taken a wholly unjustified interest in our luggage, and I was pleased when we were safely seated in the carriage and on our way to Mrs. Forrester's house. Once there, and in the house, we went to our rooms to rest and prepare for dinner. As I waited for Mary, I looked out from our first floor window, for the rain now gave place to a sharp thunderstorm, with thunder and lightning. At once, I hardly believed my eyes, as I saw there, by the fence, a figure of a man. Who could be out there in this weather? Convinced that my eyes had deceived me, I stared out, saw nothing and prepared to turn back and let the curtain fall. Just then a brilliant flash of lightning lit up the whole scene, and I clearly saw the Gypsy who had been at the station. What was happening here? What was he up too, in this dreadful weather, and why was he here now? In the same moment I felt Mary's light touch, and she said, "Is something the matter?". I turned, took her in my arm and said, "No, dear, all is well. I thought for a moment I had seen someone out there/" I tried to sound as natural as possible. "What, in this weather? You must have been mistaken," said Mary and looked doubtfully at the pouring rain outside. "Yes, I think so too. Let's go downstairs." With these words we went down to the dining room, where Mrs. Forrester awaited us.

It was however difficult to concentrate, during and after dinner, on the conversation. The picture of that Gypsy was constantly before my eyes. Where such persons appear, caution is always to be advised. Many are harmless, but it is a well-known reality, that some would rather steal a shilling than earn a guinea. Then, a single Gypsy may well be dangerous, because the reason he is alone can be that he has been banished from his family, and is now dependent on his own wits to survive. I was therefore seriously disturbed, and the situation troubled me. Equally, however, he might by morning be far away. As I did not wish unnecessarily to trouble the ladies, I resolved to say nothing. I would however ask the servants to verify and secure all doors and windows, and I knew that it might be a restless night.

A gruesome discovery

Next morning looked to be the start of a beautiful summer's day. A cloudless sky promised sunshine, the storm had passed, and all seemed calm again. I felt my concern regarding the lurking and disturbing Gypsy. If he had troubled me last night, there had been no further disturbance. I was satisfied that he had wandered off to find somewhere where he might find an easy booty and avoid recognition.

After breakfast, Mary and I determined to make a picnic outing. We invited Mrs. Forrester to join us, but she graciously declined, explaining that there were things to be done at home. We set out shortly after one o'clock, with a well-stocked basket and a woollen blanket. We followed the High Street, and just past the Wellings' house we turned to cross the stream. I had determined to visit the abbey ruins, as I was sure that this most romantic situation would interest her. As we crossed the bridge, I looked down with the thought that it was only days ago that I had met Mrs. Brown there and learned of her tragic circumstances. Now there was nothing unusual under the bridge, except to note how the stream was swollen by the previous evening's rain.

As I had hoped, Mary was delighted with my choice of picnic place. We spread out the wool blanket, between remains of the ruins, and made ourselves at home. After lunch we stretched out on the blanket and lapsed into daydreams. The warm, bright sunshine fell directly on us, and as I closed my eyes, I felt Mary move closer to me and nestle in my left arm. Her head lay over my heart, and I stroked her arm. The warmth of the sun around us, the singing of countless birds, and the sound of the flowing stream, led soon to a serenity which was filled with peace and contentedness. Mary relaxed in my arm and I heard how her breathing became quieter and slower. A glance showed that she was indeed sleeping. I smiled, closed my eyes again and dozed contentedly beside her.

I do not know how long we lay thus, nor what it was, but some different sound had awakened me. Before opening my eyes, I knew we were no longer alone. This is an instinct, a warning of potential danger, well known to every soldier who has had contact with an enemy. I cannot explain it better, but I know well that more than once, in Afghanistan, I thanked my life to this instinct. Slowly I turned my head, to see that Mary was still peacefully asleep. Behind her I saw stone ruins, mostly overgrown, but no more. I waited a moment, in case there was movement. There was nothing. After a pause, I turned my head to the other side. There were only more remains of old walls, and I could, from where I lay, see nothing beyond. Now however I heard a faint but regular sound, just beyond. With this I was wide awake. I moved Mary's hand to one side, on to the blanket, and withdrew my hand, without waking her, from under her head. Now I could cautiously sit up and look over the ruined wall. What I saw, was at first scarcely to be believed. It was the unexpected, and still disgusting, Gypsy of the previous evening!

He was kneeling in a slight dip, and appeared to be digging with his hands. What could he be doing? I stood up as quietly as I could, but he must have heard something, because he suddenly turned towards me. Screwing up his eyes, he stared at me aggressively. Since my attempt to approach him discreetly had now failed, I resolved to take the offensive, and called out to him. “You, there, my man, what are you doing?” Instead of giving an answer, he leapt up with a surprising energy, and ran off, down an old forest trail. I tried to follow, but he had a start, and he moved very fast. I might have followed on the forest track, but he leapt away into the bushes. In the thickly wooded hillside he leapt over obstacles, even a fallen tree, like an antelope, where I would have had to clamber laboriously. Thus it was that he was quickly out of sight.

Feeling defeated, I returned to the path. Mary, now wide awake too, looked at me amazed but also rather troubled. “What has happened, John?”

“I was chasing someone.” Mary asked, incredulously, “But who, then?”

“It was the Gypsy from yesterday evening.”

As I said this, I realised that I had not taken Mary into my confidence, and that she was right to look at me in bewilderment. I could only now explain. “Do you remember how I said that I thought I saw a man in the rain, by the fence surrounding the garden?"

"Yes, I do, John, and I also remember how you then said you thought you must have been mistaken."

"Mary, you are right, and that was, I must admit, a white lie. I did not wish to alarm you or indeed Mrs. Forrester. I tried therefore to keep my observation to myself, but now I can be completely open with you, and tell you that the stranger I saw last night was just this Gypsy whom I have just seen, digging there in the hollow. And as I called to him, he ran away"

Mary followed my glance towards the hollow. "But what might he have been doing?"

"I do not know, but we can go to find out. Come with me, and we will see for ourselves".

With this, we went over to the place where the Gypsy had been digging with such energy. He had opened up a hole which might at some time have been a badger sett. We went on our knees, and I slowly began to dig in the soft sand. Only a few handfuls of sand had been moved before I felt something hairy under my finger. I dig gently and carefully further, and drew a hairy bundle out of the hole. It was the body of a large dog, some forty pounds in weight. The body was long and muscular, with a firm straight back. The legs were quite short, and although the dog had clearly been dead some days, and buried in this hole, the coat was still full and silky, close to the body, and a little longer around ears, legs and tail. In the summer sunshine, the coat gleamed golden.

As I looked at all the features of this animal, Mary asked, "John, do you know what caused the death of this dog? Might it be, that he followed a badger, and was killed by it?"

"No, Mary, that was not it."

Before I could explain, she asked again, "Perhaps it ran down the hole and could not get out."

“No, Mary, that was also not so. Someone has broken the poor dog’s neck.” I showed Mary how the dog’s head could now be turned freely.

“But John, that is dreadful. Who might do such a cruel thing?”

She looked from me to the dog, which I was holding in my arms, and suddenly said “Look, John, there is a collar. Perhaps we can see to whom it belonged. Perhaps someone is missing him and is already anxious.”

“Yes, Mary, we should see. Can you perhaps release the collar?” Mary leaned over and tried to release it, struggled at first, and had to plunge her hands deep into the furry coat. As she released it, a finely made and silver ornamented collar came to light. And indeed, there was hanging on it a metal plaque with engraving. We both looked and Mary took it to look at what was engraved. Suddenly shocked, she looked again at me, and I saw that the words would not come.

“Come, Mary, what does it say?”

“Oh, John, here is engraved, ‘Chelsea.’ We both were silent, the same thought in our mind.

“That is the name of the Wellings’ dog.”

A more serious situation

With this dreadful discovery, our happy and carefree picnic was now of course at an end. Mary packed up the picnic basket, and I laid the blanket over the body of the dead dog, and secured the corners with stones. The location of the poor beast could thus quickly be found. Saddened, and deep in our own thoughts, we set out to go home. I had intended to call in at the Wellings and to give them the dog-collar. Albert, their gardener, was, however, at the gate, and so I spoke first to him. He told me that Mrs. Welling was unfortunately quite ill, and not to be disturbed, and that Mr. Welling was again in Hastings for his business matters. I resolved therefore to settle my affairs with Albert, who would surely deal with them for the best. I showed him the dog-collar. He immediately responded, with a cry, "But sir, that is Chelsea's collar." He looked at me in surprise, and I saw a look in his eyes which asked how I should come to be holding it. I explained to him that we had found the body of a dead dog by the ruin, and that we had recovered this collar, and recognised the name. Exactly what had taken place, I kept to myself.

“Oh, sir, they will be very troubled. Especially the young gentleman, he has grown up with Chelsea, and they were always inseparable. When he comes home from boarding school, the death of Chelsea will be a hard blow for him to overcome.”

“How long had Chelsea been missing, then, Albert?”

“It was last Tuesday evening, and we thought she was on one of her typical hunting trips. She was an incomparable hunting dog, with a fine nose, such as we seldom find. Chelsea would often make an evening walk in these grounds, and then pick up a scent to follow. That could go a long time, but she was always back next morning, often with the game in her mouth. That is what we thought last Tuesday, but when she didn’t come back, we feared something might have happened to her.”

“Well, Albert, if I have to be the bringer of bad news, I am at least pleased to be able to put an end to the fear and uncertainty,” I offered.

"Oh, sir, for your trouble and concern we are truly grateful. I thank you, on behalf of the whole family. I will now go over to the ruin, and bring Chelsea home." He turned to go, and took his leave, when he had a thought, and took up the conversation again with a deep sigh. "It is really such a shame, Chelsea was a beautiful, clever and courageous dog. If she had been here on Saturday, I am sure there would have been no break-in."

"A break-in," I asked.

"Yes, sir, someone seems to have attempted a burglary, because the outside door from the garden to Mr. Welling's study was broken open, and yet he seems to have been disturbed. He doesn't seem to have taken any money or valuables, but everything was in a terrible mess. All the drawers and cabinets seem to have been turned out."

"That really seems strange, Albert. But is there any idea who it might have been?"

"Unfortunately not, sir, but I have my suspicions. I don't know if you've heard, sir, but several people have seen a Gypsy hanging around in the village in these days. He seems an unusual one, quiet, keeps to himself, but he turns up everywhere. Forgive me sir, but I wouldn't put it past him. He has surely picked out the houses which stand alone around the village. It would be a kindness to warn Mrs. Forrester, before he gets to her place." I thanked Albert for his surely well-meant warning, and we saw him prepare to go off to the ruin, in order, as he put it, to bring Chelsea home.

Mary and I walked silently back, each deep in thought about all that we had seen and heard. I saw from her expression that she was clearly deeply occupied with questions. Suddenly she asked me if I really felt the Gypsy had broken in at Wellings. "I don't know, Mary, but I think there is much to suggest it. That he has been looking all around, we have seen for ourselves. And that nothing valuable is missing, is perhaps only to be explained, in that he found the wrong room. You see, Mary, he broke into the study. Anything of value is surely kept there by Mr. Welling in the safe. To break open the safe requires rather more than the hands of a Gypsy. If he had found the dining room, there would at least have been silver cutlery and table silver."

Mary looked at me in wonder. She suddenly said, "My goodness, John, you sound sometimes just like Holmes." I had to tell her that I took that as a compliment, and she assured me that it was so intended. Now she laughed again, and we walked on again in silence.

Aft a while she again broke the silence. "John, do you think it really was the Gypsy who might have killed the dog?"

"Well, I cannot prove it, but I certainly think so." She asked me why. "To do such a thing needs a lot of strength, and what is perhaps more important, a complete lack of scruples. Going by his outward appearance, our Gypsy might meet both requirements."

"But if he killed the dog, why did he have to bury it in a badger sett? And why would he be digging it up again? That seems to make no sense."

“Well, I have at least a theory. Let me explain it to you. On Tuesday last week I suspect that the Gypsy first attempted to break into the Wellings’ house. This attempt was disturbed by Chelsea, who drove out the thief and chased him over to the ruin. Here the thief turned on the dog, which paid for his courage with his life. As the thief had then broken the dog’s neck, he saw the valuable collar, and set about removing it. But he might have been disturbed, and in haste, dropped the body into the badger-hole. Today he came back to secure the silver-embossed dog-collar.” When I had finished, I looked at Mary.

“It sounds plausible, John. But if so, why did he wait until today to come back? Can you answer that?”

“I think so. As he pushed the dog’s body into the hole, he tried to cover it with loose sand. Afterwards he could not find it, as all around there is loose sand but as it rained so heavily in the night, the sand over the hole was washed out and he was then easily able to find it again.” Mary thought for a moment, and suddenly agreed, that it was very possible. She then, however, went very quiet and thoughtful.

After a few moments she said, "Oh, John, how relieved I am, that the Gypsy this afternoon was quicker on his feet than you could have been." This irritated me a little, as I could not follow her thoughts. I thought rather that I had failed, and that my body, so ill-used in the past, was simply not now able to respond when the need arose. What did she mean?

I asked her rather abruptly what the remark was intended to convey. "Oh, John, don't be offended, I was not trying to humiliate you! I was only relieved that you could not catch up with him." I was still not clear, and asked her again. "I would have thought it was clear. If he is as strong and brutal as you say, and could break the poor dog's neck, what do you think he might do with anyone who stands in his way?"

As Mary said this, she looked at me with such a look of affection and care that I understood at once. She was right, I never thought of that. The encounter this afternoon could have had a most unpleasant outcome. We remained silent for a while, and then followed a full and energetic conversation. I had this time broken the silence, and I now told Mary about everything that had troubled me during these last few days.

There had been the abrupt and extraordinary change in the Wellings, and then the encounter with Mrs. Esther Brown, the landlord's account of the three monks, and my own feeling that something menacing was all around us, and about to break.

Now there came today's events, the threatening and violent Gypsy, the dead dog, and the break-in at the Wellings. I told her of all my fears, my misgivings, and my doubts, and kept nothing back. As I ended, I awaited her reaction. I thought she might try to quiet and to reassure me, and to tell me that I had let my imagination run away. But I had misjudged her. During my account she had slowed her walking pace, and now she stopped to look first at the ground, and then at me. She was searching for the right words, and now she spoke, affectionately but with a warm authority. "My dearest, if only you had taken me into your confidence sooner! These days must have been very hard for you to bear."

I was greatly relieved by her words, and took her into my arms. "I love you, Mary."

“And I love you, John,” she said, with a depth of warmth and gentleness. Then we stood, for a moment, holding one another.

We must really have stood there for some moments, only becoming aware as several passers-by seemed to accord us an improper degree of interest. It was time to go home, and Mary asked what I was now intending to do. She spoke of the threatening events, and the sense of danger, imminent and hanging in the air. “To be quite frank, I really don’t know, Mary. I think I feel most like writing to Holmes and asking him to come and see for himself. And yet, I could not bear to bring him here for nothing, and to expose myself to ridicule.”

“John, you should not hesitate; your fears are certainly not absurd. And you know that Holmes welcomes mysterious secrets and puzzles. He will surely be pleased, even grateful, to have a matter before him which challenges his mind.” I resolved to write to him at once, but Mary’s word was stronger. She insisted that I send him a telegram, which would be quicker. With a smile, and with the feeling that we were now pulling together, we went to the railway station, where the telegraph office was located. The air was stuffy, even though the window was open. My telegram to Holmes was short, but I was sure that it would have the right effect:

Holmes

Situation becomes more acute. Dangers everywhere. Need your help – please come quickly.

Watson

I had a feeling that telegrams were rarely dispatched from Robertsbridge, although the railway company was obliged to offer this public service. The clerk made much of pulling his equipment towards himself, and reading out my telegram in such a voice that one might think it was by his vocal chords alone that the message would reach London. Since, however, I did not want to share such a message with others, I looked around to ensure that we were alone in the office. Fortunately, there was no-one else there. I thought no more about it.

As we left the telegraph office at the station, and strolled back to Mrs. Forrester's house, I felt quite pleased with myself. Holmes would surely soon arrive, and with his careful observations and deductions he would be able to resolve the whole mixture of unusual circumstances. I felt secure for the first time in days. Had I only known that the Gypsy had been leaning on the wall below the open window of the telegraph office, I might however have felt somewhat differently.

The Three Monks

On arriving at Mrs. Forrester's, she asked us whether we had enjoyed a good day. We had of course to tell her, first about the gruesome discovery of the Wellings' dog, and then of the Gypsy, the warning that Albert the gardener had given us, and my own observation, that the Gypsy had even been spying around Mrs. Forrester's. Not surprisingly, this troubled her, but as I told her of our telegram, asking Holmes to come at once to Robertsbridge, she found again her reassurance. She insisted that Holmes would be her guest, and at once gave instruction for his room to be prepared.

During the dinner, conversation strayed once more to the mysterious and disturbing events which these days had brought to light. When I asked Mrs. Forrester about the three monks, she said that she had heard the legend, but had never herself seen them. I became, during the evening, uneasy about this curious story. Was there really such an apparition, or was here some kind of collective suggestion at work? That I would have to see for myself! It would certainly be best if I had something definite to describe to Holmes when he arrived.

While the ladies prepared to leave the dining room to go into the lounge, I was coming to a decision. According to Peter, the landlord at the public house, the monks were always seen in the nights after full moon. I made up my mind to go up there now, to wait in the bushes, and to see what this was all about. When I told the ladies, they were properly doubtful. "Would you not rather wait until Holmes arrives?", said Mary.

To answer her, I tried to keep my voice as calm and unconcerned as possible. "Come, my dear, I only intend to see this play-acting for myself."

Mary was unconvinced. "It sounds very dangerous."

I tried to explain that it could hardly be dangerous to see more closely something which could only be a human game, because it was manifestly absurd to imagine there might be a supernatural power at work. That was as improbable as the stories about a curse on those who saw them. The question was only, how did they do it? Mary looked at me as doubtfully, and fearfully, as before. I really did not wish to hurt her feelings, but I could not let this matter go by me. A decision made was, after all, a matter of honour, and I could not now go back on it. As we sat there, Mrs. Forrester suddenly asked if I might like to take the Army revolver of her late husband, which, she explained, had been lying for years in the writing desk. "That is most thoughtful of you, Mrs. Forrester, but I think that will not be necessary. As I said earlier, I am only going to observe, and certainly not to take action."

I deliberately said this clearly and slowly, so that Mary would understand that I was not intending to be careless. I then said, somewhat more lightly "And in any critical situation, I always have my walking stick with me, and that has a very stout knob." Mrs. Forrester, as I intended, smiled at me, but Mary, wide-eyed, still looked pale and troubled.

"Perhaps you might loan me a dark lantern?" I asked Mrs. Forrester. She rose at once to give an instruction, leaving Mary and myself alone together. Mary still said nothing, and her silence was painful to me. I could not, and would not, leave her here without an understanding.

I spoke directly to her. “You know, Mary, that I really must try to understand what is happening?”

“Yes, John, but I am so concerned for you… do promise me that you will avoid any risks”. I promised her solemnly, that it would be so, and kissed her on her hands, which she held tight clasped together before her breast. “Oh, John, my dearest…” and she suddenly put her arms round me. We only noticed Mrs. Forrester as she discreetly coughed, and we smiled at one another. Confidence was restored, and Mary and I were at one, so I could go out into the summer evening calm and assured. With the lantern and my walking stick, I left the house.

Although the moon was no longer full, it still gave a good light. I would scarcely have reached the hill unobserved, had fortune not favoured me with banks of cloud which gave me their protecting shadow. Moving carefully, I was soon able to reach the bushes and the bank at the foot of the hill. Here I took up my position. After our visit to Hastings I even thought of the magic lantern, I was firmly convinced that the appearance of the three monks was somehow achieved with optical trickery. The realistic lantern images led me to believe that my expectation would now soon be confirmed. The time passed slowly, and my nerves suggested to me that it was time for a cigarette, but I could not risk that the glow might betray me. I therefore settled down, like a hunter in his hide, to wait, however long it needed. This was, however, more than simply an exercise in patience. I realised that my cramped position, imposed by the need to keep below the bushes, was making me stiff, and this would soon become painful. It would then not have needed much, and I might have given up my vigil, but all at once I caught a glimpse of white.

The white patch in the moonlight came nearer, and I saw that there were indeed three monks, in white habits such as the Cistercians wore. They came out of the woods, and now walked slowly through the clearing. Their hooded heads were bowed down, as if they were deep in prayer. I had to admit that, although I am a person of scientific training and conviction, their appearance left me shaken. That simple or unschooled villagers might be so afraid as to avoid the hill, and any contact with this apparition, was all too understandable. My observation point was however well chosen. The three monks came quite close to me, and I had now to admit that this was no trick of optical deception.

It was the smell of their burning torches which finally convinced me. These had to be real persons, and I was sorely tempted to step forward and ask what this was all about. There were nevertheless three of them, and I would surely have come off the worst, in which case I would never find out what this deception was designed to conceal. I thought for a moment that perhaps even Peter Hunt, the landlord, might be behind it, for he had in his own words admitted that he was perhaps the only one to profit from the story. But I wanted this time to make sure, and so I remained still, until the three monks had moved away, and then I would follow them. That should not be difficult, as the recent rain had softened the ground. The three monks were, after all, of flesh and blood, and would leave footprints.

An hour went by, feeling like an eternity, before they moved away. The three monks then turned back towards the woods and disappeared. Now I could act, and follow them. I stood up carefully and stretched my aching legs and back. I was reaching down for my stick and the dark lantern, when I was pinned down by two strong arms, and was ready to scream out for help, although I knew no-one in Robertsbridge was likely to come. And the three false monks were still in earshot, but who were they? It was hopeless, for in that very moment I lost my chance to cry out. The unknown attacker behind me held my mouth tightly closed, and I struggled, choking, to breathe through my nose. My heart was racing dangerously, and then I recognised on his left wrist the leather band which I had last seen on the arm of the Gypsy. A wave of horror went through me. He held my arms fast to my side, and I struggled in vain to break his grip. I was using my strength, and my lungs were burning for air, as I started to lose consciousness. There rose before my eyes the picture of the helpless Chelsea, her head falling freely to the side.

But now, through my wildly struggling senses, there came suddenly the clear and calm voice of Mary, saying to me, "What do you think the Gypsy might have done, to anyone who stood in his way?" I had no strength left, and I was ready, expecting the inevitable. I stopped struggling, and fought only to recover my breath, I felt how, as the attacker saw my weakness, his grip around my chest was eased. I lay still, trying to give the impression that I was already helpless, unconscious even. The moment I felt him relaxing his vicious embrace, I rammed my elbow with all my strength into his stomach. Such a blow is most painful, and I had caught him out. He recoiled instinctively, with a tormented groan, and I was free. He clutched his stomach and his face was contorted with pain. I had to act fast. I fell on my stick, grasped it and lifted it over my head for a heavy blow.

A familiar voice rang out. "Watson, stop, once like that is enough, I have no wish to come to terms with your stick…" I froze, even as I was ready to strike, and looked in astonishment at the figure still bent double on the ground before me. I had heard Holmes' voice, but was this Gypsy really Holmes?

My head reeled and I had to ask helplessly, "Holmes, is it you?" The Gypsy sat up slowly, and attempted to smile. "Yes, Watson, I am really here, and I would be grateful, if you would now put down your stick and stop threatening me". Only now did I realise that I still held the stick high over my head. I let it fall, and leaned over to Holmes. I was delighted to offer him my hand and take him in my arms.

"Please forgive me, Holmes, that I caused you pain."

"That is forgivable, Watson; it was my own fault, for I had already attacked you."

"And I must admit that you had me almost beaten, but why did you not identify yourself beforehand? We might have avoided this struggle from the start."

"My dear friend, there was neither time nor opportunity. You were on the point of endangering more than one life, including your own."

"Then I really don't understand," was all I could say. I was completely confused and could only bring out a string of questions, to which Holmes made at first no reply: "Endangering? What is the danger? And whose life was I endangering? Yours? And what are you doing here in

Robertsbridge? And why are you disguised as a Gypsy? Holmes, what is really going on?"

Holmes remained silent, and then said thoughtfully, "A most ingenious and refined, but also unscrupulous and evil crime is being pursued, and it is still not clear how it will end. But this is not the place to discuss it. Let us now go together to Mrs. Forrester's house and talk about it there."

Reviewing the Mystery

On the way back to the country house of Mrs. Forrester, Holmes made a diversion to a lonely and broken-down shed, scarcely visible in the now deepening darkness. This shed had, he explained, been his home over the last few days. I looked with some incredulity at the fallen roof and the rotting wood of the walls, and tried to imagine what he had had to suffer in order to pursue his enquiries. He was away some time, and I was deep in these thoughts, when he returned to me, and I heard him say, "Please do not be concerned about my well-being, Watson, I was not very comfortable, but I learned a great deal."

Even here, in the night, Holmes was still able to read my innermost thoughts and answer my still only half-formed questions. While I had been reflecting on this miserable hut as a shelter, Holmes showed how well he had arranged his affairs. He had already used the time to let fall his disguise, wash quickly, and dress afresh. He was determined not to arrive dirty, in his Gypsy clothes, even in the dead of night, at

Mrs. Forrester's, to speak before the ladies. We arrived there shortly before midnight.

The house was still lit, as the ladies waited nervously for my return. They were both greatly relieved and more than happy to greet me, apparently unharmed, as they both welcomed me with open arms. But how much more were they completely surprised to find Sherlock Holmes following me. After a rather confused but friendly greeting, Mrs. Forrester told Holmes that there was already a room prepared, and that he could use it at once. He accepted gratefully, but the others wanted of course to ask him all kinds of questions. He had to explain, however, that he could say little about the mystery itself, as the case, as he called it, was still unclear. He could not comment on it. He only made very clear that it was of the greatest importance, for the success of his task, that no-one in Robertsbridge should learn he was here. With this he had of course in no way satisfied their curiosity, but Mary and Mrs. Forrester were both aware that they had already become a part of his plans to frustrate a crime, and they now determined to go to bed. Mary looked at me, to see if I would follow, but I saw that she understood that I must at first stay, as a friend, with Holmes to share his concerns.

It was thus at about half past midnight that we sat together, and shared the study of the late Mr. Forrester. Holmes asked suddenly me outright: "Would you not rather first go to bed and rest, before we talk tomorrow?"

"My dear friend, what do you imagine? Since we met an hour ago, I am full of unanswered questions. I could surely not rest until we have at least looked together at some of them." I saw how a smile came to Holmes' lips, but then it disappeared just as quickly.

"My dear Watson, not least thanks to your two most informative letters, I now find myself on the trail of a most refined, carefully prepared, and at the same time callous and cruel crime. But before I go into the facts with you, I have to ask you a question." I looked at him with curiosity and impatience. He spoke slowly and thoughtfully, and searched for his words. "Watson", he began thoughtfully, "you have so often accompanied me on my cases and adventures, and have never feared the dangers which might be involved. You have always stood by me. I ask you now, if you can do that again."

Holmes' warm words moved me deeply, for I knew they came from his heart. "My dear friend, I will of course accompany you, whenever and wherever you need me. Take me with you."

The smile came back to his lips. "Dear old Watson, always a man of action. But I have to warn you. This affair is full of dangers. It might be that we fail. And even if my plan is successful, I cannot be sure that we will be in time to prevent a tragedy."

"Holmes, you are speaking in riddles. And with the best intentions I cannot see what you mean."

"Watson, I first wanted to say that we could, if we fail, be in a most disagreeable position. Angry citizens, the sensational press, and many more, would fall on us. I do not even speak of our legal situation. I cannot consider putting you in such a situation without at least warning you. These are also reasons for asking you, again, whether you still want to be involved with me, when the consequences are so unpredictable."

I saw at once that he was considering not only me but, since my marriage, also my duty to weigh such decisions as they affected both myself and my wife. He knew however that, with all love to Mary and concern for her well-being, the friendship which bound us was not to be put in question.

I had thus no doubt about the solemn weight of my assurance, as I answered Holmes and looked directly at him. "Holmes, I am proud and grateful to be called your friend. I will go with you in your task, and I will support you as well as I can. Whatever may be said about me later, I will know that we are struggling to see justice done. And should we fail, I can help you to carry that too."

"My dear old Watson! I thank you for your support, and I promise that I will do all in my power to protect you from adverse consequences if I should fail." He was silent for a moment, and closed his eyes. Then, he breathed deeply, and opened his eyes, to speak with his accustomed vigour and determination. "But we are not yet beaten! We still hold the reins of this affair in our hands".

With this, he paused again, and then began, calmly and clearly, to explain the situation, just as if we were in our room at 221B Baker Street. "First of all, I must describe to you certain facts which are an indispensable background to this affair. In order that you can draw your own conclusions, I present them in the order in which I became aware of them." With these words he leaned back, laid his fingertips together, and closed his eyes. I leaned back and eagerly heard his account.

"You will certainly recall Mr. Hall Pycroft. He had long looked for employment, and found at last an opportunity to take up a position at Mawson and Williams, the well-known stockbrokers on Lombard Street. Just before he was to start work there, he was approached by a man named Arthur Prime, who offered him the position of manager of the Franco-Midland Hardware Company, at its head office in Birmingham. This most tempting offer was accompanied by some flattery and also a certain derogatory criticism of Mawson and Williams. Mr. Prime thus persuaded our Mr. Pycroft that he should, without waiting to give notice in London, at once go to Birmingham, where he would be introduced into the nature of the work by Mr. Prime's brother, Harry. Mr. Pycroft noticed very quickly, on arriving, however, that the similarity between Harry and Arthur Prime was, even for brothers, too close to be convincing. At this moment Mr. Pycroft wisely came to consult me. I think, Watson, you will recall the case." He paused to look at me.

"Yes, Holmes, I do indeed," I replied. "I recall it well. It was shortly after our marriage, and you visited and told us something of it. I had the honour of being present when, in the last act of the drama, you exposed Arthur Prime as the well-known forger and burglar, Thomas Beddington. He and his brother were well known to the police, as they always worked together. They had done so this time too, as Thomas Beddington made out to be both Arthur and Harry Prime, while Samuel Beddington, claiming to be Mr. Pycroft, went to start work at Mawson and Williams. He was looking for information to be used in a subsequent burglary. The burglary was in fact attempted, but prevented by a courageous watchman, who however, lost his life. Scotland Yard soon caught up with Samuel Beddington, and as it was probable that he would be hanged, Thomas Beddington attempted to take his own life. We arrived just in time to prevent him from doing so." I concluded and looked at Holmes.

"Good, Watson, I see that you remember it quite clearly. Do you know what became of the Beddingtons afterwards?"

"Ah, Holmes, there I must fail you. I was fully occupied with my new practice."

"Of course, and I must tell you what followed. Samuel Beddington was convicted of attempted robbery and murder, and taken to Newgate, where he awaited his execution. The lawyer representing Thomas Beddington succeeded in ensuring that his client was only charged for fraud. The failed suicide attempt of Thomas was seen by the court as remorse for the evil deeds of his brother, so that he only received a mild sentence. The court allowed him expressly to be held in

Newgate, so as to be near to his brother in the days before the execution."

Holmes paused again, and looked with interest at me. He seemed to expect an observation, but as I did not know what was to come, I could only say that although it was a generous gesture of the court to let him be near his brother, they were both unscrupulous villains. They had had no pity for their victims. Moreover, Thomas was thereby surrounded by hardened and cruel criminals, and their influence cannot be underestimated. The likelihood was, as it seemed to me, that the courts would yet, in coming years, have time to regret that they took this course. Holmes smiled briefly, and continued his narrative, but first, to my surprise, commented: "We will not have to wait so long." I looked at him again in anticipation.

"In Newgate Gaol, Thomas Beddington became friendly with Bill Harper. Harper is well known as a smuggler, and since a difference of opinion with one of his band, which ended in the latter's death, he was also convicted of murder. It appears that Harper soon became, for Thomas Beddington, practically a substitute for his brother. They became inseparable, and, some six months ago, they succeeded in escaping together."

"Have they been recaptured, or does anyone at least know where they might have gone?" I asked.

"They were not caught, and the police think they are still in London. I do not think that is so."

"Why not, Holmes?"

"Because two known criminals, on whose heads the Crown has set a substantial reward, cannot remain concealed for so long, in the London underworld, among all who might betray them"

"Perhaps they have separated."

"It is always possible, but it is not likely. There is a connection between the two, a little like that between the lion and the hyena. The hyena has to stay near the lion, if it is to survive. Had they separated, I am sure that the police would soon have had their finger on Thomas Beddington."

"And you, Holmes, do you have an idea where they might be?"

"As I was not concerned with their flight, I only had at first a very general idea of where they might have gone. Now, Watson, I know precisely."

I looked at him in surprise. "And where are they?"

"In East Sussex"

Again I looked at him in surprise. He began to explain. "Thomas Beddington never had a real home. He went wherever his brother went. He was always at home there where his brother took him. He has surely done the same again. He will only feel safe where Bill Harper feels safe. And that must, as I soon realised, be in East Sussex."

"And Bill Harper, why is he safe in East Sussex?"

"Because this was his home from his earliest childhood. He was born in Hastings and grew up there. His detailed knowledge of the district is great, and it certainly grew as, with his father, he became a smuggler."

"My goodness, when I think that a few days ago I was strolling in Hastings with Mary, and we might there have unwittingly met Harper or Beddington!"

"No, Watson, you would not have done so!"

This remark was irritating. How could Holmes speak with such certainty? I asked him outright, "And why should that not be possible?"

"Because Bill Harper and Thomas Beddington have not left Robertsbridge during this time." In complete astonishment I looked up and stared at him.

My thoughts in confusion, I needed a moment before I could express any more than amazement. "Here in Robertsbridge? Surely that is impossible. How could two strangers succeed in hiding unnoticed, here, in a village like this?"

"Oh, they have indeed worked out a clever and ingenious plan, but I will tell you more about that later. First, if you agree, I would like to continue my description of the events in their proper order."

Naturally, I was curious to know more and to have a direct answer to my question. I knew, however, that Holmes had to follow a logical pattern in his account. When that was disturbed, then he was also disturbed, and would withdraw into himself, and continue in silent reflection. There was no choice, therefore, but to control my curiosity and to exercise patience, as I listened to his ongoing account.

"The next significant event was a fire three weeks ago, at the Fairbanks paper-mill in Emmett Street, in East London. Perhaps you saw the report in 'The Times?" Holmes looked questioningly, but I had no recollection of the event, and seeing no connection to his earlier remarks, could only shake my head.

"My interest in such a fire would, like yours, Watson, not perhaps have been aroused, had I not known that Fairbanks' mill is renowned for the quality of its paper. For example, they are suppliers to Her Majesty's Stationery Office and the Royal Mint. Emmett Street is on the Isle of Dogs, not far from the West India Docks. Being near the river, the fire was rapidly brought under control, and the production in the mill was not greatly affected. The warehouse, however, in an older building, was more seriously damaged."

As Holmes paused again, I had to admit that the significance was still not clear. I asked outright, "But Holmes, what has a fire in a dockside paper mill to do with Bill Harper and Thomas Beddington? Fires break out at this time of year in London often merely because of the summer heat. Was it then merely an accident, or was there more behind it, perhaps someone who had an interest in causing it?"

"That is exactly the question I ask myself, Watson, the more so since I visited the premises just after the fire. The floor was still covered with ashes and charred paper. On the wall which ran parallel to the Thames, however, there were stacks of paper which had not suffered greatly, in part scarcely singed, perhaps because they were first to be quenched with water. I investigated these more closely, and found that although they were soaked with water, there was an unmistakeable smell of something highly combustible in the air around them."

"Then you are satisfied that something was used to start the fire deliberately?"

"Quite so, Watson."

"And what does Scotland Yard think to that?"

"I was led clearly, and in the friendliest way, to understand that this had been investigated, and that the fire was clearly accidental. This building was older, and had no gas lighting. There was natural daylight, from the windows, but paraffin lamps were always available for work at night or by bad weather. Scotland Yard was of the firm opinion that a defective window glass caused the fire, and that the smell came from spillage from the stored lamps, which burst in the heat."

I had to admit that the official verdict sounded convincing, but I could not deny out of hand Holmes' theory of arson. I could not tell him that his idea was absurd, and left him to develop his argument further, occupying himself first with the question that if arson were indeed in play, who might have had an interest in the crime? I therefore asked outright, "Holmes, who could profit from such an act?"

"At first, Watson, I thought that this might be an insurance swindle. That however was clearly not the case." I felt relieved that he spoke in this way, apparently confirming that it was not deliberate. But his next words opened up a much more sinister perspective. "I asked myself, who might have an interest in a fire in a warehouse full of high quality paper. There occurred at once to me an obvious answer. A thief, wanting to obtain such paper, could use the fire to cover his tracks. After all, who would know afterwards, how much paper had been burned?"

“Why, though, would anyone wish to steal the paper?” and then it struck me. “But of course, Holmes, I see now that you were already thinking of Bill Harper und Thomas Beddington, and that they would want paper if they were to forge shares or banknotes. Do you really think that might be so?”

“I do indeed, Watson, and you should also know that a burglary took place at a former water mill on the river Rother, just near us here, near Salehurst, two months ago. This had housed a printing works, now closed, which was broken into, and at first it was not considered serious; the works had had to close down some time ago, and all was now locked and, as was thought, secured against entry. I learned that there had however been several forced entries. I am now certain that Bill Harper und Thomas Beddington have acquired there a printing press, materials and typesetting equipment, suitable for their plans.” Holmes stopped again, and drew out his pipe and tobacco pouch, to stuff the bowl. While he did this I began to face the possibilities he had described. I had to agree that his hypothesis was eminently plausible. Knowing that Beddington was a capable and gifted forger, it would be a brilliant idea to rob the paper mill and conceal his actions by starting a fire. Even so, it struck me that in one respect the theory was incomplete.

He was about to start again when I interrupted him with what I considered to be a serious objection. "That is an impressive conclusion, Holmes, but it seems to me that you have left out something important."

"Really, Watson? What in your opinion have I overlooked?"

"Surely the printing of share certificates, and above all bank notes, demands special inks. But so far you have in your presentation of the case made no reference to any theft of printing inks." Holmes allowed himself a slight smile, before he answered.

"My dear friend, that is a most perceptive remark. I have indeed said nothing about the need for ink. But in two respects you are mistaken. I have, first of all, not overlooked the question; rather is it in fact at the centre of my investigation. And secondly, and this is a more serious aspect than your opinion of my thoroughness, I know that the two criminals already have since some days ago an adequate supply of a special printing ink."

He observed my surprise, as I burst out with "You said nothing of that, Holmes!"

"Of course, Watson, I know, but the fault there is your own, with your anxiety to reach a premature conclusion!"

Of course he was right, and since I could not dwell on it, I quickly asked, "When did the pair of villains steal the ink?"

"Watson, I regret to have to say that they did not have to steal it. It was made available to them, or, more precisely, Mr. Welling placed a barrel ready in his depot in Hastings, for them to collect."

I looked again at him in complete unbelief. "That is surely impossible, Holmes, I have met him, and he is a most honourable gentleman. He would never stoop to being involved in a criminal affair." I was very disturbed, and

Holmes appeared to be quite unconcerned, drawing quietly on his pipe. Was he making fun of me in this most sensitive matter? My next question was "From whom have you obtained this most grotesque accusation against Mr. Welling? It is deeply insulting to him."

"I first learned it from you, my friend." I was speechless, and could only stare at him. Holmes with his sense of theatre and drama was obviously quite at ease, and savouring the moment. I was greatly relieved when he spoke again. "Watson, I have more than tested your tolerance and understanding. It is time to put all the known facts in order, and to tie all these loose threads together. Allow me to summarise."

With these words he took his pipe in the right hand, and counted off on his left hand the aspects which were important to him.

1. In prison at Newgate, the smuggler and murderer, Harper, befriends the weak and unstable forger, Beddington, and takes him under his wing.

2. Together they escape, and their hiding place is in East Sussex. The last fourteen days they have been in Robertsbridge.

3. Two months ago they were able to steal a suitable printing machine, and various accessories required for type setting.

4. Three weeks ago, at the fire at Fairbanks' paper mill in London, they succeeded in obtaining a large amount of high value paper.

"Now, with all this background information already in my hands, I received your first letter. You described the peaceful, even idyllic conditions around you. But, Watson, you know my suspicion of the perfect and peaceful country life. It is in such surroundings easier to hide the most gruesome crimes than it would be in London, where every alley has its share of inquisitive eyes and ears. Within a short time, your second letter arrived, and I was, therefore, not greatly surprised. I must truly thank you for your precise and detailed account. My dear friend, your description had perfectly caught the changes in your surroundings, without any attempt to dilute them with your own interpretations."

Holmes again drew on his pipe, and I knew that my face betrayed already my pleasure, that he could say this to me. I had naturally still no idea what he had, in my letter, found to be so interesting, or what conclusions he had drawn. But at least I had been able to help him. Now he continued. "It was clear from the change in the Wellings that something had occurred which had thrown them quite out of their ordered routines. But what might it have been? It was your most interesting conversation with Mrs. Brown which gave me an idea. "

As he again paused, I had to reflect that this must be some sort of confusion, for if one thing was clear about Mrs. Esther Brown, it was that she was a seriously mentally disordered person, on whose statements no reliance could be placed. Holmes had again read my thoughts, for he smiled again and explained. "No, Watson, you are wrong to think that her conversation is worth nothing. Admittedly, she did not herself know what she had seen and heard, but preferred to seek the explanation in her concern for the tragic death of her son Georgie. That made her account more confused. It was however just that account which served as a basis for further enquiries."

It was late, and I was impatient, and Holmes still spoke such nebulous terms that I could not follow him. I broke in, with "What then had Esther Brown seen?"

"The desperate attempt of Robert Welling to escape from his kidnappers."

"But Holmes, that could not be! Robert Welling, as a result of some misdemeanour, was still at boarding school."

"That was the story, put about by Mr. Welling, to give a plausible explanation for his son's failure to return. It was indeed a good idea, since he had to keep from any public knowledge the disappearance of his son."

"But then Mr. Welling told me a deliberate lie, as I asked about Robert?"

"Yes, Watson, he did, and I urge you to forgive him, for he was in a terrible dilemma. The kidnappers had told him, in the note which conveyed their demand for the special ink, that if he did not respect absolute silence, he would not see Robert alive again."

"But how can you then know about it? Has Mr. Welling despite everything asked for help?"

"No, Watson, Mr. Welling was not prepared to take that risk. He could not. You know yourself from your visit to the Seven Stars, that nothing can be kept quiet in this rural surrounding. Mr. Welling knows that too. He told nobody about it. My knowledge of the content of the blackmailers' letter was obtained by my breaking and entering at the Wellings home, last Saturday night." Gradually a picture began to emerge, and the confused thoughts and images in my mind began to find their place. I was still struggling, also with all this new information, when Holmes went on with his account.

"I fear, Watson, that I have departed from my logical and chronological presentation. Let me go back to your second letter. You described a sense of threat, which you felt after the change of attitude at the Wellings, and particularly after your meeting Esther Brown. I was expecting that before long Harper and Beddington would make themselves known to the Wellings, probably in writing. The suspicion arose at once, therefore, that this had been the moment, and that Robert had been kidnapped to compel his father to hand over a barrel of printing ink. My suspicion became more certain, after I made a visit to the boarding school in Tonbridge, where I spoke to the headmaster of the school, a Mr. Warren, to ask after Robert Welling. I made out that I was a distant relative, long located abroad, visiting from overseas, and in London while settling some business affairs. I said that I was looking forward to making a surprise visit to Robert and his parents, but was not sure whether I would find Robert at home or at the school, of which I had been informed. Mr. Warren was quite open, and told me that Robert had left shortly before the end of term, to return to Robertsbridge. He had himself conducted the boy to the station, and seen him onto an agreed train."

"Does that mean," I asked, "that he was travelling alone?"

"It does indeed, Watson. Mr. Warren told me that Mr. and Mrs. Welling had intended to come to the school in their own carriage on July 2nd to fetch him. Mr. Warren had then however had a telegram telling him that Mr. Welling could not leave Hastings, on account of urgent business matters, at that time, but would still like to know that the boy was safe with his mother in Robertsbridge. He therefore asked that Robert be sent home with a certain late afternoon train, and that he would there be met by Mrs. Welling and brought home.

"Since Warren knew that Mr. Welling had his own business, which made demands on him, he was not in any way in doubt. Apart from that, what harm could come to the boy in a short journey from Tonbridge to Robertsbridge? The shortcomings of the South Eastern Railway are well-known, that they are unpunctual, have poor rolling stock and yet demand exaggerated fares. But they do at least deliver their passengers to their destinations. No, I make no reproach to Mr. Warren. He had no reason to suspect a deception."

“But, Holmes, that suggests that the kidnappers were fully informed about the Wellings’ plans. Was there someone in the household who was untrustworthy?”

“No, Watson, that was not needed. You will recall yourself, how pleased Mrs. Wellings had been, that Robert was coming home, and talked of their arrangements. Your wife and Mrs. Forrester were certainly not the only ones to be in their confidence. And then think again, how you had learned that nothing in this village world can long remain a secret.”

“Yes, Holmes, you are right. Many would have known about it. But how do you think they succeeded in kidnapping him?”

“Here I can only present a hypothesis, but I can give it to you if you are interested.” I was indeed, and I assured him that it was so. “Now, Watson, these trains are not long, I think Thomas Beddington could join the train shortly after Tonbridge. He could find Robert in his compartment and join him there. He may have engaged him in conversation to gain his confidence. Whatever he did, it was enough to prepare for the next stage."

"Do you think that was enough for Robert to go with him?"

"Surely not, but a sense of friendly confidence was surely needed. Robert was however certainly not likely to go of his own accord with a stranger, even a friendly one."

I nodded my agreement. "I would rather think", continued Holmes, "that Beddington was able thus to administer some kind of sleeping draft, perhaps even with a sweetmeat or confection. At Etchingham, the last station before Robertsbridge, he then alighted, taking the boy with him, and if any passengers or railway staff saw them, they would have seen the two, the boy obviously tired and sleepy, and thought no more of it. But there are so few passengers that even that is not sure.

"At the station Bill Harper was waiting with a wagon, and in minutes they would be on their way, perhaps throwing a blanket over the sleeping Robert, the better to conceal him. On arriving in Robertsbridge, they turned up the lane to the abbey ruins. Now I suspect that the drug was wearing off, and that he was coming round. As he recovered consciousness, he looked out from under the cover, and saw that he was close to home. He jumped up, sprang out of the wagon, and shouted for help with all his might. Bill Harper stopped the wagon and went after him, quickly overpowered him and dragged him back. There was however a witness to all this, and that was Mrs. Esther Brown, who, however, was not in any position to know what she had really seen and heard." Here Holmes had again to pause and draw on his pipe.

Then he continued, "But now we come to another drama. The dog Chelsea was on the grounds at the Wellings, as always in the evening. Chelsea heard the cry for help, knew at once that it was Robert who was in need and had shouted, and chased up to the ruins where the wagon had now gone. I think she must have attacked Bill Harper, trying to get Robert free. This is characteristic of the breed.

"You may recall, Watson, that I had a case where the character of various breeds was most relevant. I could find no textbook which met my needs, and so I had to collect my own notes for a small monograph. I can assure you, therefore, that the Sussex Spaniel is a first-rate hunting dog, which can search out on its own all sorts of game in thickets, undergrowth and reedbeds. It is a loyal, friendly and lively companion, but it can also follow a scent in almost any ground, needing no guiding hand. Chelsea had however against Bill Harper no chance, for he broke the dog's neck and hid the body in an abandoned badger sett. The kidnappers went then to the abbey ruins, in part of which a blacksmith's smithy, had been built."

Holmes drew again on his pipe and I took the opportunity to ask another question. "And are Bill Harper and Thomas Beddington still there?"

"Yes, Watson, they have made themselves at home, and have installed their printing press in the stable of the smithy."

"But Holmes, however have they achieved it, that they can work there undiscovered and undisturbed?"

"That, Watson, is the doing of the three monks. As you know, the local population was always afraid of the haunted abbey. They keep well away."

"But that means that the three monks are part of the affair?"

"Quite so, Watson; Bill Harper, who knew the legend of old, because of his childhood here, has arranged that they should appear, as a warning."

Here, then, at last, were the three monks, whom I had now seen, and of whom a village was kept in fear. Slowly the pieces of the puzzle were coming together, and they were forming now a more complete picture. I tried to order my thoughts anew, and Holmes closed his eyes, put his hands together and appeared at once to be sleeping. I felt that it was surely time, for I knew that he would have slept little in the time he had been in Robertsbridge. And yet… I still had one more question. I had to ask, even at the risk of disturbing him, for I knew that without it I could find no peace of mind. "Holmes, where is now Robert Welling? Is he still a prisoner?"

It was a moment before Holmes answered. His eyes remained closed. "As a Gypsy, I was able unobserved to get nearer to the old abbey, in that part where the smithy had been built. I watched Bill Harper and Thomas Beddington as they were printing their forged notes. Of Robert Welling there was no sign. I have also not seen either of them leave the smithy at any time to go to a place where Robert might be held."

"But he must be there somewhere?"

"Yes, Watson, but I fear the question may be not only where, but….." Holmes opened his eyes, and I saw his pain as he continued. "The question may now rather be, whether he still lives."

"But Holmes, why should they kill him?

“Firstly, because he has seen them, and secondly, because he is no more use to them, now that they have what they wanted, the special printing ink, from Mr. Welling.”

“But they would have to be unbelievably callous and cruel to kill a defenceless child.”

“Yes, Watson, we may think so, but Bill Harper has already murdered. His moral inhibitions are certainly not to be trusted. When I think how he broke Chelsea’s neck, I would not entrust myself to his mercy.”

I looked at him anxiously. He spoke slowly again. “The kidnapping of Robert Welling is a dramatic and dangerous element in the whole affair. Had it only been a question of arson, burglary, and forgery, I would have put it all in the hands of Scotland Yard. But now it is different. The well-being of the child is in the forefront of the whole affair. Now, as long as we know no better, we must consider that Robert still lives, and can be saved. That is why I have been so careful, and why I have waited, while making myself familiar with the abbey and its surroundings. But time is now pressing."

He had again made me curious, and now things were again unclear. "Why is time now so pressing?"

"Because, Watson, in your second letter you told me how Peter Hunt, the landlord at the Seven Stars, poetically expressed it, when he said that they all knew that the monks only appeared between the full moon and the half moon. From full moon to half moon is normally eight days. They can only rely on the legend, and fear of the haunting, during this period. Full moon was on July 1st. The day of half moon, July 9th, is the day after tomorrow. Bill Harper and Thomas Beddington only have tomorrow to leave Robertsbridge, that is, up to tomorrow night. Since we must have them to find Robert, we need to act tomorrow night."

"Holmes, do you already have a plan?"

“Yes, but I will explain it to you tomorrow,” replied Holmes. “First you must get as much sleep as you can, because you will need it tomorrow.”

“And you, Holmes?”

“I will stay here for a while, with another pipe, so that I can go through tomorrow’s measures once more in my mind.” As he said this, he began to stuff his pipe again. I looked at him somewhat thoughtfully, wondering if I might leave him here in Mr. Forrester’s study. He certainly needed sleep more than I might have done. He gave me no choice however, as he saw my doubt. His look brooked no contradiction. Then, he smiled, and said simply, “Good night, Watson”.

I knew then that I could do no more. He would now withdraw into his own thoughts, going through his whole plan. I could expect no more from him. There remained only, however hard it might seem, to wish him a good night in his turn. I succeeded in slipping quietly into bed beside Mary, in the hope of quickly going to sleep. It took however some little time, before my tiredness, indeed, exhaustion, took over from my racing thoughts.

The Plan

As I awoke next day, I realised that it was already late. The bed beside me was empty, and looking round the room I saw that Mary must have been up some time, had dressed and was most probably now with Mrs. Forrester. I washed quickly, dressed, and went down to the ground floor. Mary, Holmes and Mrs. Forrester were in the dining room, obviously waiting for me. They greeted me and I joined them at the breakfast table.

A first glance at the two ladies made clear to me that that Holmes had already informed them, at least in part, of the circumstances. During breakfast, he made no further reference to the matter, but showed himself to be a charming and entertaining guest. Conversation ranged over the violin concerto he had recently attended at the Albert Hall, and the Reading Room of the British Museum, which he had used on so many occasions.

The two ladies enjoyed a light meal, while Holmes and I were served with a substantial breakfast. As soon as this was at an end, however, the ladies attempted to learn more of Holmes' plans, and hear what he intended to do next. He was however, as on the previous evening, not prepared to talk about his intentions, excusing himself by saying that from now on, only complete secrecy could assure the success of his plan. Naturally somewhat disappointed, the ladies decided to withdraw for the afternoon to the garden. Holmes and I went again to Mr. Forrester's study. Well established with cigars and whisky, we then settled into Holmes' description of his plans.

"My dear friend, it will not have escaped your attention, after my account yesterday, that we are in a most uncomfortable and even threatening situation."

"I think I have understood, Holmes. The problem is that we know that a criminal act has been performed, but that we can do nothing without endangering the life of young Robert Wellings."

"Quite so, Watson. Should we call the local police, we would have to tell them what we know. At first, most probably, they would not believe us, and we would lose valuable time. Then, when the police finally begin to act, it will perhaps be too late to save young Robert. I fear, moreover, that they would act in such a way that the real objective might be missed."

"And that is?"

"To catch the kidnappers alive, so that they can tell us where they have hidden him."

"Of course you are right, Holmes, the boy's safety comes before everything else. It could well be an error to rely on the local police. But perhaps we should ask Inspector Lestrade or Inspector Gregson for their help?"

"Well, Watson, those two are perhaps the most capable in Scotland Yard, indeed, perhaps the only ones with clear sight when others seem blind, but it would not help. Once they were informed, they would be obliged to mobilise the police responsible for Robertsbridge. That must end up with the storming of the old smithy, and then there would be afterwards little hope of finding Thomas Beddington and Bill Harper alive."

"But Holmes, what then can we do?"

"We will use a trick."

"A trick? What then?"

"Before you can understand that, I must explain what I have learned about the three false monks. As you realised yesterday, they serve our two kidnappers as a diversion. This was so, not only during the time that the forged notes are being printed. It was already so beforehand."

I looked at Holmes in surprise. ."You will consider, Watson, how the two criminals had to install the printing press, in the old smithy, and bring up the special paper they had stolen, the printing ink, and also Robert Welling, all of which had to be unnoticed."

“Are we then dealing in fact with a band of five persons?”

“Not really, Watson. And here we can use the circumstances to act.”

“ I’m sorry, Holmes, but here I fail to follow you.”

“What I have found out is that the three monks were in fact hired by Bill Harper. They have otherwise no connections to him.” I obviously looked sceptical, because Holmes went on: “It is really so, Watson. My researches as a Gypsy showed me that they are in reality three brothers, John, Michael and Thomas Critton, who live in the small village of Salehurst, a short distance northeast of Robertsbridge. They are small-scale smugglers and have in the past worked occasionally with Bill Harper. This time they were engaged by him, but the Critton brothers seem to know nothing of the forgery; they believe there is a smuggling operation, for which they are providing cover. “

“And are the Critton brothers living with Harper and Beddington at the smithy?”

“No, they pursue their own activities around Salehurst by day, but come over to the smithy in the evening, and are given three monks’ habits by Bill. When their performance is over, they go to the smithy, give back the three habits, collect their pay and go back to Salehurst.”

“And they do that each evening? “

“Yes, Watson.”

“But is that not remarkable? I can imagine that Bill doesn’t want his business to be known by any more persons than necessary, but don’t they want to know more about the bigger affairs they are being called to conceal?”

“I suspect that Bill Harper’s reputation is the reason for their lack of curiosity. He was always known to be dangerous and unpredictable, and now, after he murdered one of his partners, he is treated in his circles with the greatest respect.”

"All the same, it is surely a source of danger to the two accomplices, to have the Critton brothers twice each evening at the smithy. That must surely too easily be observed."

"It is indeed surely a risk, but you must remember that the people of Robertsbridge go in fear and trembling of the monks. I also saw how the Critton brothers do not use the highways, but take various footpaths across the fields, between Salehurst and the ruins. They go across country, and they obviously know the terrain very well."

"I see, Holmes, but how are we to use this knowledge?"

"It is my plan, that when the three brothers have finished their act on the hill, we will intercept them and bind them securely. I will then, with two companions, all dressed as Cistercians, go in place of the Crittons to the smithy. If this works, Bill Harper will come out of the old smithy to pay the brothers and collect the habits. At that moment we can gain entry, and overpower Bill and Thomas Beddington."

“Holmes, that sounds excellent. But you spoke of two companions. I hope I am one of them.”

“Your enthusiasm is most encouraging. I had hoped that that would be your reaction. But be aware: despite all caution, we might still fail. We must fear that if we fail, we will not save Robert Welling.” Holmes paused, and I saw him deeply moved. After a short pause he added bitterly, “And it may be that we have already waited too long, and that he is no longer alive”.

Enthusiastic as I might have seemed, my heart felt heavy at that moment, as I felt my friend’s last words settle upon me. It was a while before I felt ready to break the silence which lay upon us. “Holmes, we will not think of that. We will first turn your plan into action. May I ask who the other companion might be?”

“Naturally, Watson. My choice fell on Mr. Welling.”

I looked at Holmes in surprise. “Do you think that is a good idea, Holmes? I can understand that you do not wish to have more persons involved than absolutely necessary, but is Mr. Welling not too much involved, emotionally, to be able to give us useful support?"

"I consider, Watson, that that is precisely why he can help us to success. When he knows the situation and has heard what I intend to do, I think he will recognise that this is the only chance we have to save his boy's life."

I did not entirely share Holmes' confidence, but it was his plan, and he must know how he intended to carry it through. I therefore resolved, not to ask further, but to ask instead: "Have you already made an approach to Mr. Welling?"

"Not yet directly, but I have sent him a note by messenger boy. When he has seen it, I do not doubt that he will come at once." It was not long after this, that we heard at the house front door a commotion of impatient ringing and hammering of fists. Mary, Mrs. Forrester, Holmes and I all went into the entrance hall, and the servant opened the door a crack. It was enough to allow the heavy figure of Mr. Welling to burst into the hall. His face was ugly. A mixture of anger, fear, anxiety, rage and bitterness left nothing to doubt. His one hand was clenched to a fist, while his other clutched a scrap of notepaper. He stood in the entrance hall and looked, in turning round, at each of us, and finally fixed on Holmes. He raised his hand holding the note, shook it and demanded in a breaking voice, “Sir, can you tell me what this is about?”

The atmosphere was confused and frightening, until Holmes’ voice broke in firmly and clearly, “Please follow me, Mr. Welling. Then I can answer all your questions.” With this, Holmes went directly to the study, and Mr. Welling followed him without a further word. Mary and Mrs. Forrester look at me, enquiringly, but I did not know what was in the note, nor did I know how the conversation between Mr. Welling and Holmes might develop, I could only make a gesture, with my shoulders, and, leaving them there, follow the others into the study. They were already seated, and Holmes asked me to give Mr. Wellings a whisky. As I gave him the glass, he opened wide his eyes and, full of anxiety, asked me again, what all this meant. He opened his hand and gave me the note, and I recognised Holmes' clear and striking handwriting. The message was:

If you wish to see your son Robert alive, come at once to the house of Mrs. Forrester, but do not speak a word to anyone, not even to your wife.

Holmes began. "Now, Mr. Welling, first I must thank you that you have taken up my invitation. My name is Sherlock Holmes, and I already know that your son was kidnapped, in order to oblige you to hand over a barrel of your special printing ink."

At once, as he heard the name of my well-known friend, Mr. Welling's eyes fixed in a concentrated stare at Holmes. His expression showed both relief, and, also easily observed, a great anxiety. Holmes, whose gift was to read people in front of him as an open book, did not miss anything. "Mr. Welling, you must fear nothing. I am here incognito. Nobody knows, neither the police nor others, that I am here. I have now a plan, which will enable us to apprehend the kidnappers and rescue your son. To put it into effect, I need both your agreement, and your assistance. Should you prefer, however, to put the matter in the hands of the police, I will give you every help to do so."

"No, Mr. Holmes, please don't do that! The kidnappers have warned me most explicitly, not to do anything of that kind. In these last days I have several times considered asking Dr. Watson here to invite you to help me. Each time, my fear of the possible consequences for Robert has held me back. But now, Mr. Holmes, without any word from me, you obviously know about the affair, I can only ask you, no, indeed, I beg you, to help me".

As he spoke, Mr. Welling sank to his knees before Holmes, and raised his hands in his desperate plea for help. Holmes, for whom demonstrations of emotions were always an embarrassment, looked to me for relief. I stepped quickly to Mr. Welling, helped him on to his feet again, and led him back to his armchair. In doing so, I spoke reassuringly to him, and poured him another glass of whisky. My words had their effect, and he began, also with the whisky, slowly to relax. Holmes could now, in a few carefully chosen words, describe how he became aware of the crime, and what he now intended to do, in order to save Robert and apprehend the villains. He ended his account with the question, whether Mr. Welling was prepared to accompany us in the evening on our task.

"Indeed I will, Mr. Holmes", replied Mr. Welling, in a voice now almost as firm and strong as I had heard him earlier.

Holmes' face broke into a satisfied and reassuring smile. Then he said, "As we have a long night ahead of us, I consider it best if you would now rest as much as possible. Mrs. Forrester will surely not take it amiss, if you, Mr. Welling, make yourself comfortable on this sofa.". Holmes then stood up, and left the study. As I followed him, but before I closed the door, I looked across at Mr. Welling, who was already lying on the sofa. He seemed to feel my concern, for he looked back, turning his face to me, and nodded. His eyes betrayed his excitement as he prepared for a hunt in the coming night, and as he felt hope, at last, that the end of the affair might yet be a happy one.

The Hunt begins

Early in the evening we partook of a light dinner, so that we were strengthened for the coming night, but would not feel burdened. Mr. Welling, who had, on Holmes' advice, not left the Forrester house, joined us at dinner. The atmosphere at table was very subdued, and at the same time tense, a circumstance which was not due to the presence of Mr. Welling, but to our shared awareness of the task which now lay before us. Holmes, Welling and I were in an almost feverish mood of anticipation, while the ladies were principally concerned about our, and Robert's, wellbeing. I had already had to reassure Mary, as she realised what we were planning, that I would be very careful and take no unnecessary risks.

Shortly after eight we left the house. Holmes, Mr. Welling and I, as we set off, had a dark lantern, several lengths of rope, and the late Mr. Forrester's army revolver. We left in a northerly direction and after the bridge were soon in the belt of woodland at the foot of the hill where the monks would appear. On account of the densely growing trees, it was already getting dark here, and Mr. Welling confided to me that this part of the wood was completely unknown to him. He hoped then that Holmes had some idea where we were.

I must admit that it was more than disagreeable in this dark forest, and I would have been thankful for the lantern. The danger was, of course, that our quarry would see a light and immediately suspect that they were in danger. We had therefore no choice but to rely on the failing daylight, and to rely on Holmes as guide. In that respect it was clear that Holmes had studied and walked through these woods and knew them thoroughly. He proceeded with that same competent approach which I had often observed, when he was on the trail of criminals in London. Just as in London he made it his business to know every street and alleyway, so he had here studied the forest and now knew every tree and thicket. I am sure he could have led us blindfold.

We had already gone some way, and the terrain began to change. The woods were no longer so dense, and began to give way to a low scrub. With a gesture, barely perceptible in the failing light, Holmes halted our little group. Then he whispered to us: “This is the right place to wait for them. As you can see, some forty yards away is the clearing where the monks will appear. The smithy is east of us, so the Critton brothers will come from our left, and also withdraw in that direction. As soon as they turn to go back to the smithy, we will act.”

“Mr. Holmes”, whispered Mr. Welling, “Can we not capture them sooner? Why must we wait so long, until they finish their work?”

“Because to return too early to the smithy must arouse the suspicion of Bill Harper, and then my deception must fail, putting in danger the whole undertaking.”

After a pause, Mr. Welling whispered again, “Forgive me, Mr. Holmes, I had not thought of that. It is the consequence of my impatience to see Robert, take him in my arms and bring him home to his mother.” The last words were accompanied by a self-conscious and tormented smile, which I only saw because my eyes were now more unaccustomed to the darkness. Holmes nodded, and ordered now complete silence, as we concealed ourselves behind the thick bushes, waiting upon his order to act. As I knelt between my two companions, I could observe them both. While Mr. Welling did his best to keep his excitement under control, Holmes displayed the calm and patience of a practiced big game hunter.

It seemed already an eternity since we had taken up our position. How gladly might I have lit a cigarette, to steady my nerves, but the old soldier in me realised that even that could betray our presence. There was nothing but to wait, as must my two companions, in patience.

In that moment, and in surprise, I felt Holmes' hand and his iron grip on my shoulder. I looked at him, and then saw for myself what his finely tuned ear had already heard. The three Critton brothers were there, before us, in their white monks' habits, heads down as they walked past us, as if they were in prayer. In the clearing they lit their torches and let them swing gently. Their behaviour was precisely that which I had already observed, the previous evening, but this time the performance did not seem to last half as long. As they now approached the edge of the wood, they extinguished their torches, and walked closely in front of our hiding place. I felt Holmes' body tense, as he awaited the moment. Then he leapt up, and with a cry of "Now, get them!", fell upon the first of the three.

Mr. Welling and I did the same with the other two monks. With our advantage of surprise, it took only moments to have all three Critton brothers on the ground. Holmes ordered them to take off the habits, and they did not hesitate, as they realised that a heavy Army revolver was aimed at them to make the point clear. It was the revolver of Mr. Forrester, which I had brought up. Holmes had suggested it would be best if the weapon was in the trained hand of a soldier.

Mr. Welling quickly gathered the three habits, and we secured the three brothers hands and feet, before putting on the habits ourselves. I felt satisfied and said to Holmes, "Congratulations! The first part of the plan has worked!"

I was ready to go on to the second stage, when Mr. Welling said, "And what do we do with these three?"

“We leave them here and let the police come later to collect them”, replied Holmes.

“And if they can get free?”

“If they can do that, which I doubt, they will try to make a clean getaway. But that will not help them, as I already know their names.”

“And if they should try to get to the smithy before us, to warn Bill Harper?”

“That they cannot do. And even then, they must get there after us. You see, Mr Welling, that the time aspect is of considerable importance in our action.”

It seemed that Holmes’ explanation satisfied Mr. Welling, who nodded approvingly. We checked again the ropes securing our prisoners, and then, encouraged by our good start, set off towards the ruined abbey. Led by Holmes, we were ready to see it through. We could not have dreamed, in what cruel way this next stage could turn into a deadly drama.

In the Smithy

Thanks to Holmes' detailed knowledge, we came soon to our objective. Despite the various buildings erected around the abbey to create the smithy and stables, it was easy to see that the principal building had been a church, in the classical form of a cross. We approached the smithy from the north, and hesitated at the edge of the forest, to pull our hoods down, and shade the lantern. Then we went forward again.

Before us was the east wing, already in a ruinous condition, but the south wing looked to be in a rather better state of preservation. Holmes whispered to us that there was here a kilnhouse, as well as the stable he had already mentioned. He headed purposefully to a small door in this wing of the building. As he reached it, he struck three times on the door. Nothing seemed to happen. We kept our heads down so as not to be recognised, but now we looked up, anxious because things were not going as we had intended. Holmes struck again three times on the door. Again nothing seemed to happen, but then a faint light appeared behind a small leaded window by the door. We heard the scraping of a bolt, seemingly loud in the silent night. I felt Holmes relaxing, as the door opened a crack, but then I saw a metallic glint. Holmes, with a fierce blow to my chest, abruptly pushed me away, so unexpectedly that I fell to the ground. There was a sharp detonation, and a flash, and the next moment Mr. Welling fell to the ground with a cry of pain. Very shocked, I looked to the source of the shot, but the door was again closed and the light was gone.

"Come, Watson," I heard Holmes say, in his energetic voice, "We must get him to safety, out of the line of fire." We each took an arm of Mr. Welling, and pulled him, despite his cries of pain, into a corner, safe from sight and further fire. I bent over him and examined the wound. On the sleeve of his habit there was a red stain, already growing. We drew the habit away, and took off his jacket, and, now unhindered, I tore open his shirt sleeve. It was clear that he had received a clean flesh wound, which seemed neither to have damaged bones, nor injured any major blood vessel.

"Watson, how is he?"

“It is a flesh wound, clean through his forearm, and a good bandage will be enough for the moment. He is unconscious, as a result of the pain and the shock. Pulse and breathing are normal; he seems to be of a strong constitution.” I saw how Holmes nodded earnestly. “How could that happen, Holmes?”

“I have no idea, Watson. Something must have aroused their suspicions.”

“Did you see who fired the shot?”

“No, but this suggests more the murderer than the forger.”

“And what do we do now, Holmes?”

“You will first attend to Mr. Welling. I will go after the criminals myself.”

“But Holmes! Alone against those two! That would surely be suicidal, at least wait for me!”

"No, time is critical, now that they are warned." With these words Holmes took off the habit, now of no further use to him, and his jacket, and then carefully folded the habit and laid it under Mr. Welling's head. He then folded his jacket around his own left arm. I had no idea what he had in mind, but I was very fearful for his well-being.

"Then, Holmes, please take the revolver with you," I said

"Come, Watson, you know we must take them alive; if they are dead they cannot help us. It is better that you take the weapon. If, for any reason, I cannot apprehend them, then it will be your turn, my dear friend, to resort to this last extreme."

I knew he was right, and I also knew that I could say nothing to hold him back. I could only say, "As soon as I have cared for Mr. Welling, I will follow you."

"Good, but be careful."

"Holmes, that I must even more say to you."

"Have no doubt, that is exactly what I intend. But now I will leave you."

With this, he turned back to the side door which had just brought us such a disastrous misfortune. This door was of massive wooden construction, and the bolt which I had heard would surely prevent any entry. It was therefore a mystery to me, how he intended to break into the building. Now, had I not seen it with my own eyes, I must admit that I would not have believed what followed. He took a run at the small leaded window, jumped up from the ground, and flew like a panther through the air. His left arm held up before his face broke through the glass, which shattered with the loud noise of breaking glass and wood. Once through the window, he would have to turn in the air to land on his feet. While I prayed that no ugly surprise might await him, I listened in case there were any other noise inside. I heard then the scraping of the bolt, and saw the door now thrown wide open. Holmes' athletic figure appeared in the doorway, and he waved to me. I waved back to show that I had understood. I was to follow that way as soon as I had dressed the wound of Mr. Welling.

The dressing and bandage were soon applied. I could have done this in my sleep, having, in Afghanistan, dressed the most appalling wounds, in the most adverse conditions. It was rare that an army doctor had there the satisfaction of seeing his patient recover. And each life that I might save soon became a potential victim of the next fight. I quickly learned to hate this senseless killing, the meaningless deaths and my own helplessness, which was all I could offer to stem this insanity. While I was thinking thus, my hands had already done their work; a quick check reassured me that Mr. Welling was for the moment properly cared for. I covered him with my habit, so that he would not lose more of his body warmth, and prepared to follow Holmes.

In the stable all was dark and quiet. At the back, however, I could see a faint light. I walked forward, carefully feeling my way. I could not avoid walking on the glass splinters which betrayed where Holmes had made his dramatic entry. Unable to prevent the noise, I decided to have the revolver already in my hand, as I went forward. With every step, as I went on, there was more light, and then there appeared before me the printing press which Holmes had described to me. As I went nearer, I sensed and then saw movement. With a firm, clear voice I called out, "Come out! I've seen you."

There was a short pause, and then there emerged from the shadow of the printing press a further shadow, taking the form of a person with hands held high over his head. "Come out, man, I won't say it again, out into the light!" I tried to keep my voice resolute and steady.

Obviously my words had their effect, for he emerged into the light, so that I could see that it was Thomas Beddington. He was clearly very disturbed, looked at me with wide frightened eyes, and stuttered repeatedly, "Look sir, I give up, please don't hurt me." I kept my revolver on him, and searched him for a weapon. Finding none, I put my revolver away, and took two lengths of rope from my pocket, to tie him up. In the meantime I kept a sharp watch on Beddington, in case he started any trouble, but he seemed to accept his situation almost apathetically, as on the first occasion that Holmes and I had met him.

Now, as he had been made secure, I took him roughly by his jacket and asked him where Bill Harper had gone. "He went to the kiln house, and as I saw the anger in the face of the one who was chasing him, I tried to hide here."

"And where have you hidden the boy?"

Beddington rolled his eyes nervously, and his face became even whiter than before. Then he blurted out, "A boy? I know nothing of a boy." Furious, I took him by the collar, and shook him, my right fist raised to strike him. "Oh, sir, please don't hit me, I beg you, don't hurt me."

I let my right hand fall, but held him fast by the collar. "In that case, tell me what you know".

"Sir, you must believe me. …I wanted to have nothing to do with a kidnapping. …But Bill said it was the only way we could come to the special ink we needed… And then he promised, I only had to help him with the kidnapping itself…Afterwards he would look after the boy”.

“And what does that mean?” I shook him again.

“Bill said he had hidden him somewhere nearby, with a loaf of bread and a jug of water. That’s what he told me…. And since then he hasn’t mentioned the boy. …. That’s really all I know.”

“Does that mean that Bill Harper has done nothing more for him since the kidnapping?” I was shocked and incredulous, and stared at Beddington.

He shrugged his shoulders and then said, “I really don’t know, sir,… I asked him once about the boy and he told me not to concern myself with him. He said that now that we had the special ink, the boy was of no more use to us.”

My fury over these evil and coldblooded words, even though he was only telling me of Bill Harper’s actions, was too much for me. My self-control failed, and with my right fist

I hit him hard under the chin. Shocked and hurt, he stared back at me in terror, and I tried valiantly to calm my nerves.

"And where has Bill Harper hidden him?"

"I really don't know, sir….no, truly….please don't hit me again… I don't know anything… I have hardly been outside the stable. …Bill gets furious with me…I am afraid of him when he is angry."

While he was stammering out these comments, he was looking at me with fearful, almost crazed eyes. In view of Holmes' judgment, which he had already passed on to me concerning Thomas Beddington and Bill Harper, I was obliged to recognise that Beddington really could not help us to find Robert Welling. Our only hope must be Bill Harper, and Holmes was somewhere searching after him. I could achieve nothing more here, so I went on to look for the kilnhouse.

As I was nearer to the back of the building, I found a revolver on the floor. The barrel was still warm, and the smell of smoke told me that this had been used for the shot that wounded Mr. Welling. Perhaps Holmes had succeeded in a struggle in getting Bill Harper to drop it. Again I thought of Holmes' warning, that we needed Bill Harper alive. Just then I heard noise above me, rapid steps, heavy gasping breath, and grunting, and they were somewhere over my head. Then I saw an old, decaying wooden ladder, whose rungs were already partly missing or broken. I climbed very cautiously up it, into a hayloft.

It was very dark, with just a trace of light which came mainly through the missing floorboards. The floor under my feet was obviously in the same decaying state as the wooden ladder. Two figures were struggling in the darkness, scarcely to be seen or distinguished. In a straightforward fist fight I would have had no fears for Holmes, but this was an all-out fight between these two men, with no holds barred. They went at one another like two dogs, but suddenly one was thrown through the air and hit the wooden floor hard, with a fearful grunt. I was sure it was Bill Harper, and that Holmes had used a Japanese wrestler's baritsu hold, which had, as he had often told me, helped him in the past. Even as I watched, the boards under Bill Harper's body gave way, bursting, one after another. Holmes saw at once the danger, and tried to grab him, but it was too late. The rotted floor gave way under both of them, and there was a wild scream. Then there was just a gaping hole in the floor of the hayloft.

Dust rose in a dense cloud, in the faint light from below. For a moment I stared at the hole, unable to think or act, lamed by fear, and by anxiety over Holmes. I felt icy fingers clutch at my heart, but then I fought off these feelings and found myself able to move again. Instinct said, look down from the edge of the hole, but I had to watch every step over the rotted boards. I lay on the floor to distribute my weight better, and could finally look down, where, to my delight I saw Holmes' face. My heart leapt within me. He was holding on, with one arm, to one of the beams of the roof, hanging there while attempting to reach up with the other hand.

"Hold on, Holmes," I called, "I'll pull you back up." I reached with both hands for his arm, and uttered a quick prayer that my shoulder, ruined by a shot in Afghanistan, would hold long enough, and that the boards would hold the weight of the two of us. Tensing my muscles, I lifted with all my force and slowly drew Holmes up to the hayloft floor. We lay exhausted side by side for a moment, and then crawled carefully back to a stronger part.

As we once more felt a solid floor under us, we sat up and again breathed deeply. Holmes recovered first, and said, "You cannot imagine how relieved I was to see your face above me, old friend."

"That I can well believe, for I felt the same when you pushed me out of the line of fire by the entrance, and there was no opportunity to thank you."

We were silent for a moment, and then Homes asked, "Have you found Thomas Beddington?"

"Yes, and I left him securely tied up by the printing press. He insists that he has no knowledge of where Robert Welling might be. I fear that he is speaking the truth."

Holmes nodded earnestly and said bitterly, "Then we have now no way to find out where the boy has been hidden."

"But Bill Harper… did he survive the fall?"

"That he definitely did not!" And Holmes' face, as I asked him, showed his bitter disappointment.

"Holmes, are you really sure?"

Instead of an answer, he threw back an abrupt question. "Haven't you seen what was stored downstairs, beneath us?" I could only shake my head. All I had seen, through the hole, was Holmes. "Well, then, let us go down and see it for ourselves."

Holmes and I carefully descended the decaying wooden ladder. He now led me gently to the part of the barn where the hole in the floor above was now visible. Here, in a corner, old agricultural machines were stored. Bill Harper had fallen on one of these, and Holmes said quietly, "We used to call this a hay tedder, for turning the newly cut hay to dry, but I never saw anything like this." Harper's body had been pierced, as he fell on the machine, by several of the protruding metal spikes which turn the hay. Several streams of blood ran down his torso, forming a spreading pool on the ground. It was a disgusting and shocking sight. Most of all, however, I was struck by a feeling of helplessness and anger. One look at Holmes showed that he had felt the same reaction. Each of us was thinking the same.

The only person who could have taken us to Robert Welling will take his secret with him to the grave.

The Hiding Place

Each of us stood there, silent with our own thoughts, beside Bill Harper's lifeless body, for what seemed a long time. As the silence became too oppressive, I could no longer endure it and spoke: "Holmes, whatever can we do now?"

He did not, or could not, answer. He turned abruptly on his heel, and went back to the printing press. I followed close behind, and saw as we came to it that Thomas Beddington was still securely bound where I had left him. Holmes looked at him critically and asked him directly, "Where are you holding Robert Welling?"

"I really don't know....Bill had hidden him, sir, really, sir, that's what I told this other gentleman." His frightened stare went between me and Holmes, back and forth. He kept repeating that he knew nothing of where the boy had been hidden, and how he had not asked further, because of fear of Bill Harper.

Holmes was irritated by the pleas and denials of our prisoner, and turned away from him. He closed his eyes, and held his lips so tightly pressed together, that they formed a thin line. As he opened his eyes again, I saw that he had made a decision. He spoke again. "First of all, we must get Mr. Welling to Robertsbridge, best of all to Mrs. Forrester. For that we will use the two horses and the waggon which Beddington and Harper have kept at the other end of the stable. We will take Beddington with us."

"As you say, Holmes. But what about Robert? Should we not search for him?" I saw that Holmes was struggling to keep calm at the thought.

"Of course we must search for him, Watson, but we cannot do it alone, that is a quite impossible undertaking. Just in these stables and around the kilnhouse there are countless hiding-places, not to think of the west wing which was at one time the house of the abbot, and is now a farmhouse. And then in the surrounding woods – again, there are innumerable possibilities to hide the boy. Just think of all the holes, caves and even abandoned huts such as I used. No, a hunt on this scale is too much for us alone."

"Does that mean that you will have to call in the police?"

"Yes, Watson, I have no other choice. From Mrs. Forrester's, I will go early to the telegraph office, and inform Lestrade. He can then take all necessary steps. In that way, we will quickly have a search party." With these words, Holmes went away to the far end of the stable, to find there the wagon and horses.

We first unloaded the packed bundles of forged banknotes which had been stacked in the wagon. After Holmes had harnessed the horses, we carried Mr. Welling, who was still unconscious, to the wagon and laid him on its deck. We released the rope round the feet of Thomas Beddington, so that he too could climb up and sit on the floor. I took my place beside Mr. Welling, so that I could help him in emergency, and Holmes climbed up to the driver's bench and took up the reins. He urged the horses on, and we quickly reached the house of Mrs. Forrester. Despite the night hour, we found the house lit up and Mary and Mrs. Forrester waiting for us, to learn what we had done. Thomas Beddington was, with the servants' help, soon locked in the cellar, and the two house servants then carried Mr. Welling to an empty room on the ground floor. I now dressed his wound more thoroughly. Mary helped me as I did so. I told her what we had done during the night, and I saw her fear as she realised what we had been through.

While Mary and I cared for Mr. Welling, Holmes took the carriage to the telegraph office at the railway station and sent off two telegrams. One was to Scotland Yard, and the other was personal, directly to Inspector Lestrade. As soon as he returned in the dawn light to the house, he recounted briefly to Mrs. Forrester what had happened. As he concluded, Mary and I left Mr. Welling. "How is it with him, Watson?" asked Holmes at once.

"The injury is not serious. He should soon come round." Holmes did not answer, but nodded his thanks.

Mrs. Forrester spoke again. “Perhaps we should send for Mrs. Welling, to come here, so that she is with him when he comes round”.

We all looked at Holmes, expecting a reply or a comment, but he seemed not even to notice us. He was at the window, looking out. The first rays of sunshine signalled the start of the new day. After the years of our close friendship, I knew what he was going through. He had committed all his energy and strength to the task, to save an innocent child. He had held back the results of his enquiries, as he thought, in the child’s best interests, and now it all seemed to have been in vain. Most probably we would now never find Robert Welling, and even if we did, we would only find a dead child. Holmes would have to explain and justify his actions, for the parents, perhaps before a court, and certainly before the sensation-seeking press. I was sure he could not have done otherwise, but there would be many who would be happy to discredit him and ruin his life. This picture before me pulled again at my heart.

Instinctively, I moved nearer to him, and answered Mrs. Forrester's question in his place. "That is certainly thoughtful, Mrs. Forrester, but is it not also too much for you? We are already a regular invasion here in your household."

"Please do not be concerned, Dr. Watson. I am only too pleased when I can help you all. Perhaps, however, it might also be valuable to invite the vicar, Reverend Crane, to join us. He knows the Wellings well, and can surely help them."

"I think that is a first-rate idea, Mrs. Forrester, thank you for the suggestion."

She smiled and replied. "Then I will do that at once".

She left the lounge directly to give instructions, and Mary went with her. As Mary passed me, she said quietly, "John, you must help Holmes. He looks fearfully depressed."

As Holmes and I were alone, I stood behind him and laid my hand gently on his shoulder, while I said, "Holmes, you need not reproach yourself. You have acted in the best knowledge and with a noble conscience." He did not reply, but I could feel, in his heavy, pained breathing that he was sorely tormented by his thoughts.

Around three quarters of an hour later the vicar arrived in his trap. I had just looked once more at Mr. Welling, as he came into the entrance hall. He again, as before, started to talk profusely.

"Oh, Dr. Watson, I am so nervous, now that I have the privilege of meeting Mr. Holmes personally. I would surely have been one of the happiest of men on God's earth, were it not for these terrible circumstances. Mrs. Forrester has told me that Robert Welling had been kidnapped, and that Mr. Welling is wounded. Is that really so?"

"Yes, indeed, Reverend Crane, and I would be very grateful if you could look after Mr. Welling, and also his wife, who will be arriving at any moment."

"But of course I will, Dr. Watson, of course." He paused, hesitatingly, and I saw that he had something on the tip of his tongue, which he was anxious to say, and so I looked at him to encourage him to continue.

"Oh, Dr. Watson, do not think my question amiss, even though it may seem absurd to you. Do you think, please, that I could just meet Mr. Holmes and shake him by the hand? You know already how much I admire him!" My first reaction was that this was not a good idea, because Holmes was in such an exhausted, depressed and defeated mood at this moment. But then I reflected that the admiring attentions of the vicar might just help him to bring him out of his lethargy. I therefore led the vicar into the lounge, where he respectfully approached his great hero. And, naturally, he began at once to address Holmes in another torrent of words of sympathy but also admiration.

"Oh, Mr. Holmes, I am so sorry. You cannot begin to imagine how moved I am, to find you in person before me. I have followed in the Strand Magazine all the accounts of your adventures, and it was long my deepest wish one day to meet you in person. I only wish the circumstances might have been different." Here the vicar paused briefly, to draw breath, or perhaps to give Holmes a chance to say a suitable word. Since my friend however remained without reaction, and still stared wearily out of the window, the vicar continued. "I had long feared that there would be trouble, as the village people again began to talk about seeing the three monks. It is they who keep the legend alive, though the legend itself is based on a historic reality. Perhaps it was the punishment of the Almighty, that believers, and especially their ministers and priests, were so persecuted in those times."

Again the vicar paused, looking expectantly at Holmes, who still showed neither the least sign of recognition, nor did he speak. I began to feel sorry for the vicar, that he received no response, and so I felt obliged to ask him a question. "Were these three monks then really put to death?" Grateful that at least one of us was showing an interest, Reverend Crane continued with his narrative.

"Indeed they were, Dr. Watson. The abbey was fallen upon in the evening by a lawless band, and that night three of the monks were pursued and put to death. The torment must certainly have gone on all night, for the three monks were reputed to have been strong young men. I have to say, Dr.

Watson, that one must feel by such proceedings that the devil himself had a hand in the doings." These last words were spoken with such a force, that one had to believe it was the honest conviction of a man of God, and as he concluded, there was a moment of quiet. I then had the sudden feeling that the vicar himself felt that this had not been quite the moment for such fierce words, as he smiled, somewhat painfully, and then continued with enthusiasm:

"And yet, even in such a moment of terror, we can learn that one should never lose the belief in our Lord. It was surely He Himself who held a protecting, shielding hand over the other nine monks, so that days later, hungry and fearful, but otherwise unhurt, they found the way to Salehurst." The vicar again paused, and looked at Holmes and myself expectantly. I was however disappointed that the vicar had not succeeded in bringing about a change of heart in Holmes. I was preparing to lead him courteously out of the lounge and back to the Wellings, when I suddenly realised that Holmes' attitude had indeed changed. Quite unexpectedly he turned on his heel, faced us both and then confronted Reverend Crane, whose surprise was complete.

Holmes' expression was still very tense and drawn, but there was a trace of a smile, and his eyes were no more visibly tired, but lit up with an almost feverish brilliance, such as I had often observed when he was off on the hunt for his quarry. Holmes seized the vicar's hand, with both of his own, and shook it strongly, while he quite suddenly said, with open heartiness, "My dear Reverend Crane, you do not know how grateful I am that you have come to see me. But there is now no time to lose!" He turned then to me, to say "Come, Watson, the game is not yet over!" With these words he hurried past the astonished vicar, to the door, and I followed him as best I could.

The wagon, with which we had come from the smithy, stood still outside the house, where the servants had secured the horses. Holmes jumped with surprising energy on to the driver's seat, and I clambered after him, having scarcely time to sit down before the whip cracked. We seemed to be racing towards the abbey ruins and smithy. "Holmes, what are we going to do?"

“We will find where the monks were hiding. I am quite convinced that that is where we will find Robert Welling.”

“But, the hiding place of the monks, whatever do you mean?”

“That is the hiding place where the nine monks of whom the Vicar spoke were able to save themselves.”

“But Holmes, the nine monks could have hidden anywhere, even in the woods. And you had yourself said that such a wide search was pointless.”

“Watson, you are quite right, and yet, we can now greatly reduce the scale of our search. Think back to the time when the abbey was attacked. The three youngest and strongest monks resolve to sacrifice themselves, to save the others. The legend tells us that they were killed on the west side of the abbey. If they were trying to divert the attackers away from a hiding place, this must have been on the east side.”

"Holmes, you are surely correct, that could well have been so. But does that really help us? On the east side is the forest, and there the problem is the same as before."

"No, Watson, I think not. They could not have hidden and survived in the woods. Nine monks, of whom one or two would surely be aged or infirm? No, I am sure there was a hiding place in the abbey."

"What, for nine persons?"

"Yes, why not, a secret room or vault…"

"And you believe that such a room has then up to this time survived undetected? It must surely have come to light when the smithy was built."

"Not necessarily, and I am in any case of the opinion that it would be in the partly ruined east wing."

"And why should that be?"

“Because there the monks had their cells, and the monks could only have hidden as long as they were unobserved when going to their hiding place.”

“What you tell me, Holmes, sounds logical. But then, even when the hiding place is where you suggest, why should Bill Harper know of it?”

“Just think, Watson, that Bill Harper has known these woods and the abbey ruins all his life. Most of that time he was a smuggler. Smugglers need safe places to hide their contraband, and it is surely not implausible, that in searching for such a place, he had at some time come upon the hiding place of the nine monks.”

“Indeed, Homes, it seems well possible. I only hope you may be right.”

“Watson, I felt that it is worth a try”.

As he said this, he halted the horses, and the wagon, as we were now in front of the smithy. We took with us the lantern which we had left behind in the night, and two heavy crowbars which we found in the forge of the smithy. As we came nearer to the east wing, my modest hopes began again to wane. By the thin morning light, it was obvious that the east wing was truly a ruin. Holmes seemed undeterred, for he entered without hesitation, on the former ground floor, and walked steadily across the paving. He looked down, carefully studying the floor, at each step, and, with his crowbar, knocked on the stone setts. Each one gave off the same dull sound, until suddenly one of them rang slightly higher and lighter. Holmes fell to the floor and felt with his fingers for the cracks between the setts.

"Watson, here, quickly, look, this stone is not set like the others, but only resting. Let us lift it with the bars and see what it hides". It was heavy work to lift the stone, for the bars had no firm grip, but finally we lifted up the one relatively flat stone. We saw that it had, like a lid on a jar, closed an opening which was not wide, but gave space for a thinner man to pass through. "I must go down to look, Watson, please give me the lantern, as soon as I am inside".

With a more than doubtful feeling I saw Homes disappear into the black hole below us. As requested, I gave him the lantern, and then it was some time before I heard his voice again. "Watson, I was right, there is down here a large vaulted room, and in the far end there is something on the floor."

I heard no more, for he again went back into the vault to look further. I waited three or four minutes, each like an eternity. At last I heard again Holmes' voice, excited, as he called. "Watson, I have found Robert! And he is still alive! He is unconscious, but be ready, I'm reaching him up to you".

My heart leapt at the news. I thanked Heaven and took hold of the boy's body and upper arms as Holmes thrust his through into the light. I laid him carefully on the ground, and went to help Holmes, but he was already climbing out of the opening. I started at once to examine the boy. It seemed to be a miracle. His small chest rose and fell almost imperceptibly, though his pulse was slow. He seemed to have no other injuries, but, considering that he had been several days in this vault, it was no wonder that he was very weak and dehydrated.

I carried him gently to the wagon, and laid him on the floor. Holmes had discovered a flask, and washed it out and filled it at the still running small fountain outside. Very carefully, I let a few drops fall in Robert's mouth. At first he could not swallow, but all at once something in him stirred, and he blinked and eagerly drank more water. Now however, the effort was too great, and he fell back again exhausted, going to sleep at once. Holmes looked at me in alarm, but I now knew and could reassure him:

Robert is alive and will now recover.

I watched over Robert, as Holmes climbed once more to the driver's seat and steered the horses back more slowly than before, to Mrs. Forrester's house. We were soon there, and, in moments, were surrounded. After our unorthodox and hasty departure, Mary, Mrs. Forrester, and the vicar, who had seen us return, ran out to the yard to see us. Their joy and relief, as they saw that we had found Robert alive, was indescribable. I told them all that he should now recover within a few days, and would mainly need rest and loving care to build up his strength.

Mrs. Forrester, who had sent word into the house, suggested, “Dr Watson, we should now bring Robert to his father and mother in their room. Mr. Welling has recovered consciousness, and Mrs. Welling is with him.”

“That we will certainly do,” I said, “But I find it would be better if Holmes could carry him.” I looked at Holmes and said, “Really, Holmes, without your efforts and your determination Robert would have been lost. And now I have to care for my dear wife and calm her assuredly troubled heart”. With these words, I climbed down from the wagon, and went directly to Mary, took her in my arms and kissed her warmly.

The vicar and Mrs. Forrester watched in wonder as Holmes took the boy up in his strong, sinewed arms, and mounted the steps into the house, followed now by Mary and myself, still with our arms around one another, and Mrs. Forrester, and the vicar. As Mr. and Mrs. Wellings saw Holmes enter with Robert in his arms, they both cried out with joy and delight. Holmes laid Robert by his father, so that with his uninjured arm, he could embrace his son and his wife.

They were in tears, with the relief and thankfulness of this moment. We wanted to withdraw discreetly, but Mr. Welling stopped us. With a deeply moving voice he said softly, "Mr. Holmes, from the fullness of our hearts, my wife and I thank you for this moment. You brought our child back to us, and that we will never forget. Speak, and whatever you would have from us, Mr. Holmes, you shall have."

Holmes displayed a quiet smile as he considered what he would say. "Mr. Welling," he then said, "Finding the solution to your problem has given me a most interesting and varied stay in the country. My friend Dr. Watson will confirm to you that I am never so content as when I have a problem to solve."

"It is therefore, in my view, not you who has to thank. Rather should I be thanking you." Holmes had in this most emotional moment found exactly the right words. We smiled with him, and quickly found, in sincere laughter together, that the tension of these days was behind us.

Conclusion

The secret of the three monks was thus explained. I would not wish, dear reader, to burden you now with the details of what followed, so I will simply present you with a summary of the conclusion of the case.

Inspector Lestrade had received Holmes' personal telegram, and had alarmed by telegraph the East Sussex Constabulary office in Battle, the nearest police station to Robertsbridge. Officers from Battle came first to the house of Mrs. Forrester, and immediately took into their charge Thomas Beddington, whom we had locked in the cellar. Holmes then took them into the woods, to the place where we had left the three false monks, the previous evening. There the three Critton brothers lay cold and hungry, but exactly as we had bound and secured them, and they were at once arrested. Holmes then led the police to the smithy and stable at the abbey, where they secured the forged banknotes and the printing plates. Finally, they recovered the body of Bill Harper, and arranged its removal.

In the meantime Inspector Lestrade arrived, in a bad temper because he felt he should have been called much earlier. However, as several criminals had been apprehended, and a serious forgery case frustrated, and the kidnapped child was now also safely recovered, Lestrade gradually calmed down. Holmes assured him, as he had already strictly told Reverend Crane, that he did not wish to be connected in public in any way with this affair, and with this assurance, Lestrade soon recovered his composure.

It may be, dear reader, that you recall how in late summer the newspapers almost all reported the successful end of a kidnapping affair, the recovery of substantial sums of forged banknotes, and the arrest of a dangerous escaped convict. Several most favourable reports appeared, concerning Scotland Yard and, particularly, the work of Inspector Lestrade and his team.

Mr. Welling and Robert recovered steadily, and were soon visibly stronger. Holmes later asked me whether, in view of Robert's ordeal, it would be in order to question him. I was able to reassure him. Mr. Welling gave his agreement, and thus Robert told us about the kidnapping and about his imprisonment in the vault. His description revealed that the kidnapping from the train had taken place just as Holmes had deduced, He described also his attempt to escape, by the bridge, and he told us how Chelsea had courageously attempted to intervene. Talking of his dog, and its tragic, violent death brought heavy tears to his eyes. When he was able to continue, he told us how Bill Harper made him descend into the vault, and gave him there a loaf of bread and a jug of water. Harper had then replaced the stone at the entrance, and that was the last that Robert had seen of him. Robert told us that he had tried himself to raise the stone, but was not strong enough. He tried to use the water as economically as possible, but it did not last long. He was most thankful when it rained heavily outside, and a stream of water found its way into the vault. He could satisfy his thirst, and at the same time refill the jug. As this report of the torment of these several days was at an end, we felt our anger rise, with the thought which struck all three of us, like a blow in the stomach, as we faced this cruel reality:

It had never been Harper's intention that the boy should ever come free. The vault in which Robert was hidden was to become his grave!

Before we later left the Wellings, Mr. Welling again repeated his offer, to meet any wish Holmes might have. My friend, however, refused once more to consider any payment. He said, however, something which moved me deeply, so much that I will never forget it. I must therefore report it here.

"Mr. Welling, I had my reward at the moment I was able to deliver your son alive into your, and your wife's, arms. If you would however grant me a wish, let it be this: Think generously of Mrs. Esther Brown. You know, from my description of the case, what a cruel blow she had suffered, but also, that without her observations I might never have been concerned with your son's disappearance. If you would like to do something for me, first explain to her that it is thanks to her that Robert now lives. Who knows? Perhaps it will have a positive influence on her confused mind. And even when that is not so, please make arrangements that Mr. Brown has enough financial support to ensure that she can remain at home in his care, so that she must never be sent to an institution".

Mr. Welling agreed at once, and once again I gained an insight, how noble and generous was the heart of my friend, just as much to be praised as his intellectual brilliance which was recognised by so many.

Following this last visit to the Wellings, Holmes announced that it was now time to return to London. As he said, in Baker Street there was work waiting for him. He was anxious to complete his monograph on the Classification of Ashes and products of combustion, and was planning another chemical test for verification of dried bloodstains. On the latter subject he hoped, if he were successful, to write a new treatise. We all tried to persuade him to take a few more days' rest in the country, but he was not to be convinced. Mrs. Forrester told Mary, as I later discovered, that she feared the real reason might be to escape from the well-meant attentions of the talkative Reverend Crane.

"Well, one could hardly disagree with him," we both said, as if from one mouth. But I, as his friend, also naturally knew that this, and indeed the unfinished work awaiting him, were not the only reasons why he wanted to get back to Baker Street. Although I knew, for example, that a certain praise and flattery were not unwelcome to him, too much personal attention simply wearied him. It was also quite typical of him that, when a case was concluded, he lost interest in it at once.

I suspected also that, though he would not say so, he realised that Mary and I would now welcome some time quietly together. I could also not forget that he loved London, with all the adventures, crimes, problems and unresolved puzzles which it offered. He would surely soon be striding out again along dark, dirty, foggy streets, ready at all times to face evildoing and cut it short.

It was well that I could not know how soon my reflection would become reality. In London an appalling crime of international dimension was already taking shape. Holmes and I would, sooner than we thought, be caught up in it.

The End

Also from Johanna M. Rieke

Do you love Cornwall, with its cliffs and breakers, sleepy fishing harbours and villages? Would you like to meet a real English Lord? And do you enjoy an authentic, well researched historical crime story? With the author you will accompany the renowned Baker Street detective, Sherlock Holmes, and his friend Dr Watson, on their journey to Cornwall. There, in idyllic surroundings, they are faced with seemingly impenetrable questions, leading to desperate villainy. A fifty-year-old history of intrigue, smuggling, betrayal, murder and revenge waits to be revealed, and you are there, with Holmes and Watson.

Also from Johanna M. Rieke

London in 1890 is shocked by a series of gruesome murders. There seems to be no rhyme or reason to them, except for their location in the Thames dockland. Scotland Yard is perplexed. Can Sherlock Holmes and Dr Watson help before worse follows? And what is really going on? Author Johanna Rieke brings rich and poor in Victorian London realistically to life, as she unfolds for you the surprising story of the Thames Murders, as disaster is averted at the last moment.

MX Publishing

MX Publishing brings the best in new Sherlock Holmes novels, biographies, graphic novels and short story collections every month. With over 400 books it's the largest catalogue of new Sherlock Holmes books in the world.

We have over one hundred and fifty Holmes authors. The majority of our authors write new Holmes fiction - in all genres from very traditional pastiches through to modern novels, fantasy, crossover, children's books and humour.

In Holmes biography we have award winning historians including Alistair Duncan, Paul R Spiring, and Brian W Pugh

MX Publishing also has one of the largest communities of Holmes fans on Facebook and Twitter under @mxpublishing.

www.mxpublishing.com

Also from MX Publishing

When the papal apartments are burgled in 1901, Sherlock Holmes is summoned to Rome by Pope Leo XII. After learning from the pontiff that several priceless cameos that could prove compromising to the church, and perhaps determine the future of the newly unified Italy, have been stolen, Holmes is asked to recover them. In a parallel story, Michelangelo, the toast of Rome in 1501 after the unveiling of his Pieta, is commissioned by Pope Alexander VI, the last of the Borgia pontiffs, with creating the cameos that will bedevil Holmes and the papacy four centuries later. For fans of Conan Doyle's immortal detective, the game is always afoot. However, the great detective has never encountered an adversary quite like the one with whom he crosses swords in "The Vatican Cameos."

"An extravagantly imagined and beautifully written Holmes story"
(**Lee Child**, NY Times Bestselling author, Jack Reacher series)

www.ingramcontent.com/pod-product-compliance
Lightning Source LLC
LaVergne TN
LVHW050648100826
845148LV00011B/2036

* 9 7 8 1 7 8 7 0 5 6 9 3 0 *